P
An

M000235584

THE ALIEN SKILL SERIES

Reader's Favorite Book Awards 2021
GOLD MEDAL WINNER - Category Preteen

Wishing Shelf Book Awards 2019-2020
SILVER MEDAL WINNER - Category
Teenagers

Feathered Quill Book Awards 2021
FINALIST - Category Young Readers.

IAN Book of the Year Awards 2020
FINALIST - Category Juvenile.

Reviews:

"The series just keeps getting better and better."

"Solid aliens-crash-to-earth tale."

"One of the most amazing series I have ever read."

BOOKS BY RAE KNIGHTLY

Prequel
The Great War of the Kins
Subscribe at: www.raeknightly.com

THE ALIEN SKILL SERIES

Ben Archer and the Cosmic Fall, Book 1
https://www.amazon.com/dp/1989605192

Ben Archer and the Alien Skill, Book 2
https://www.amazon.com/dp/1989605095

Ben Archer and the Moon Paradox, Book 3
https://www.amazon.com/dp/1989605141

Ben Archer and the World Beyond, Book 4
https://www.amazon.com/dp/1989605044

Ben Archer and the Star Rider, Book 5
https://www.amazon.com/dp/1989605176

Ben Archer and the Toreq Son, Book 6
https://www.amazon.com/dp/1989605214

The Knowledge Seeker
https://www.amazon.com/dp/1989605311

BEN ARCHER

and

THE COSMIC FALL

A boy with an alien power.

Rae Knightly

For my husband,
the real superhero.

CONTENTS

CHAPTER 1 *Missing*

Ben Archer knew that something bad had happened to him on the night of *The Cosmic Fall*. He knew this because, precisely one month after the event, he was still waking up every morning from the same nightmare. He would sit up straight on his bed, a scream stuck at the back of his throat. It was always the same. One minute he would be reliving that fateful night on his closed eyelids, the next he would be wide awake, sweat pearling his forehead, his mind grasping for the fading images.

Wednesday morning, September 27th, was no different. The alarm clock yanked the boy out of his turbulent slumber, sending the dark threads of his nightmare scattering to the back of his mind where he could no longer reach them.

A Jack Russell Terrier jumped onto Ben's bed to check on his master.

"'Morning, Tike," Ben mumbled, patting his faithful dog before sinking back into the bed. Gathering his thoughts, he searched his mind for the smallest hint of a memory. But it was already too late; whatever he had been dreaming about was already lost to his conscious mind.

The family doctor had explained that it was normal to experience temporary amnesia after having been bedridden for almost three weeks. High fever could distort one's memory and provoke terrible nightmares. Seven days ago, when the doctor declared Ben healthy again, he recommended the boy take it slow but try to get back to his normal life as soon as possible.

Whatever normal means...

Tike wagged his tail, then nudged Ben in the neck with his wet nose.

"Okay, okay, I'm up already!" Ben grumbled.

He dragged himself out of bed, and pulled on the jeans and t-shirt that lay in a heap on the floor of his messy room. He headed for the bathroom where he checked his reflection in the mirror. His cheeks hadn't fully recovered their colour, and there were dark pockets under his brown eyes. His auburn hair stuck out all over the place, as though someone had tried to vacuum it during the night. He gave his head a quick brush but had to abandon a mesh of hair that poked out from the back of his head.

Tike waited impatiently by the front door.

Ben opened it. "Hurry up, Tike. I gotta go in fifteen minutes."

The white-and-brown dog scurried down the stairs of the apartment block, then headed to the yard to do his morning business.

In the meantime, Ben filled Tike's bowls with crackers and fresh water. He poured out his cereal and milk before sinking into the couch to gulp down his breakfast in front of the TV. He flipped through the channels as he munched on the crispy cereal. 8:00 a.m. meant the morning news came on.

"...tensions between China and the US have once again escalated due to the event social media has dubbed *The Cosmic Fall*," a news anchor with a serious air reported on Channel 2. "A source from the US Defense Ministry has claimed off-the-record that the American satellite which was destroyed in space four weeks ago, was in fact, designed to spy on Chinese territory. The head of the FBI has denied these allegations and continues to accuse China of destroying its communications satellite. On a more reconciliatory note, the President of the United States has once again urged the Canadian government to grant access to the crash site to both Chinese and US investigators to help them determine the exact cause of..."

Ben switched channels.

A morning talk show came on, showing a cheerful man who held up a palm-sized rock. "...it is so compact it weighs six pounds! But wait until you hear its price tag! One pound of this meteor debris is worth over a million dollars!"

The show host squealed while the audience watching the live show gasped.

"I can picture folks frantically overturning their yards to find meteor nuggets!" the show host laughed.

Ben pressed the control again.

This time an old black-and-white image of hills covered in torn-up pine trees appeared on the screen while a soothing voice explained in the background, "Thousands of hectares of trees were crushed to the ground like toothpicks by the shockwave of the exploding meteorite in Siberia in the 1970's..."

Ben turned off the TV in a hurry. His hand shook over the control.

I should know by now not to watch the news!

He jumped when he heard a scratching on the door, his cereal spilling over the edge of the bowl.

"Darn!" he muttered.

He opened the door to let Tike in, leaving a trail of milk all the way from the living room to the kitchen. Having lost his appetite, Ben placed the half-eaten bowl of cereal in the kitchen sink. He tore off a paper towel, then roughly soaked up the milk drops on the carpet. Tike watched him curiously with his head cocked.

"Think it's funny, huh?" Ben uttered, as he scrubbed the floor.

Not a sound left the dog's throat. Ben observed the terrier sitting patiently before him.

How come you never bark anymore?

Ben picked himself up from the ground and threw the paper towel away. He put on his jacket, then flung a water bottle, banana, energy bar and a wrapped-up ham sandwich loosely into his backpack before heaving it onto his right shoulder. While struggling to zip his jacket, he headed down the hall to his mother's room, his backpack scraping against the wall. The door stood ajar so he peeked inside.

Tike joined him and peered through the crack below him.

Laura Archer lay on her bed, fast asleep. She had recently begun working night shifts at restaurants and bars after losing her day job. Her former boss had not appreciated her spending week after week watching over her ailing son.

Ben hesitated to leave his sleeping mother, half hoping she would open her eyes. He wanted to tell her he'd had another nightmare. But when she didn't stir, he whispered, "Bye, Mom," before tiptoeing away.

He put on his runners. "I'm outta here, Tike. I'll see you in a bit." His eyes fell on his dog. Tike gave him a forlorn look that dug deep into the boy's heart.

Ben bit his lip. "Oh, come on, Tike! Don't do this to me again! I have to go to school. You know that!" He knelt to hug his four-legged friend. As he rubbed Tike's back, he felt the warmth of the fur and the beating heart inside the dog's chest.

We share the same fear.

Ben stood hastily, bothered by the thought.

Out loud, he said, "Take care of Mom, okay?" He quickly closed the door to avoid glimpsing Tike's eyes again.

* * *

At the doctor's recommendation, the twelve-year-old had reluctantly gone back to school, which was a drag because he had missed the first two introductory weeks of September. One of Ben's closest pals had been placed in another classroom where he had already made firm friends with a new boy. Ben's other classmates had formed tight-knit groups; they had prepared their first homework and knew which teacher taught what. Ben felt like an outsider disrupting a well-established order.

It didn't help that he spent the first week in a daze. He had a hard time concentrating on the lessons and felt exhausted by the time he got home. His mother told him to be patient, his body had experienced a great shock and was still pulling itself together. Young people recover quickly, she would say. You will be fine in no time.

I don't think so...

As he let himself out of the three-story building, Ben took out a plastic bag to pick up his dog's poop before the downstairs neighbour could complain. He threw the waste in public garbage, then jogged down the street towards school.

Not so long ago, he would have run down the three blocks of houses without a second thought. Yet although four weeks had passed since

Ben fell ill, he ran out of breath as soon as he reached the first pedestrian crossing. He slowed to a fast pace as he hugged the walls of the houses, hunching over to fend off a sprinkling rain, and made it in time for the school bell. He weaved his way through the groups of students, intent on reaching the main door so he could get away from the outdoors and the crowds.

Something ripped. The weight of his backpack fell away from his shoulder. Catching his breath, he glanced down to find the strap had torn off. In his haste that morning, he had neglected to zip the backpack all the way. Its contents spilled onto the ground, his pens rolling over the playground, his notebook falling into a patch of mud, and his water bottle emptying itself on a library book.

Students burst into laughter around him while others pushed past in their haste to get inside. No one offered to help. Ben was left to fend for himself as he painstakingly recovered the pieces strewn around him. By the time he was done, the last couple of giggling students ran by, their shoes thumping on the asphalt.

Ben lifted his backpack with both arms to avoid any further embarrassing fabric tears. But as soon as he stood, he became fully aware of the empty playground and the immense sky above. He was alone, at the complete mercy of the emptiness, unprotected and vulnerable. His head swam dizzyingly and his vision blurred. Ben clung to his backpack for dear life. His heart raced, and his breath came in gasps as he experienced the burden of a full panic attack. As soon as he shut his eyes, the nightmare erupted without pity: a dark mass falling from the night sky, his Grampa shouting in warning, twisted eyes, the shadow of a man with white hair reflected in the fire, a whisper...

Mesmo.

Tike's snout on his cheek.

"Ben!" someone shouted, shaking him by the shoulders. "Wake up! Ben!"

He opened his eyes. Tike's paws were on his chest, the dog's face close to his own. Above him, his mother called to him anxiously. He blinked and found himself lying in the middle of the playground, surrounded by Tike, Laura, and a couple of teachers.

A school assistant ran up to them, a cellphone in her hand. "I'm calling an ambulance," she announced, holding the phone to her ear.

"No!" Laura objected. "Please don't! I'll take Ben to our family doctor. He's familiar with Ben's condition."

The assistant hesitated, then put the phone away.

"Are you okay?" Laura asked Ben, eyebrows knitted.

Ben nodded to reassure her.

She helped him up carefully. "The school called me and said you were standing by yourself in the middle of the playground. I hurried over with Tike. You were completely paralyzed." She accepted Ben's backpack from one of the teachers.

Ben became excruciatingly aware of the adults staring at him strangely. From inside the school, students pressed their noses against the windows, pointing in his direction.

Oh, great! Nice way to blend in...

CHAPTER 2 *The Dugout*

Agent Theodore Connelly entered the office of High Inspector George Tremblay, deep in one of the Canadian Security Intelligence Service's best-kept secret underground facilities, hidden in northwestern Ontario. Although only thirty-seven years old, early loss of hair had pushed the agent to shave his head completely. This gave him a handsome, clean look which went well with the job.

The High Inspector sat behind his desk, legs crossed, ankle over knee, the tips of his fingers drumming together as he conversed with a man sitting opposite him. Several files lay open on the High Inspector's desk and he closed a couple of them before standing up to greet Connelly.

The assistant in a tidy suit and skirt who had led Connelly in, gestured elegantly towards the imposing man in his early sixties. "High Inspector George Tremblay, Head of the National Aerial Phenomenon Division of the CSIS," she said, before presenting Connelly. "Agent Theodore Edmond Connelly, Chilliwack RCMP, British Columbia." She then left the office gracefully.

Connelly said nothing as he offered his hand to greet the High Inspector. The latter gestured towards the seated man with stern-looking straits. "This is Inspector James Hao. He is leading the investigation you have been assigned to. You will report to him at all times and he, in turn, will report to me."

Hao stood and shook Connelly's hand while they held each other's gaze.

Connelly took in the man's black hair streaked with grey above the ears.

The High Inspector invited both men to sit as he went through his thick files, one of which clearly contained information about Connelly. The High Inspector made direct eye contact with the bald man, saying firmly as if reading from a textbook, "Anything that is said regarding the current investigation is classified and divulging any or all information will be penalized immediately and without revoke in accordance to the law on treason to national security."

Connelly automatically responded, "Yes, Sir."

The High Inspector scanned some documents, nodding satisfactorily.

"You have made quite a stellar career, Agent Connelly," he began. "From patrolling the streets of Chilliwack for ten years, to leading investigations at the CSIS Headquarters in the past month. Your colleagues are already saying you're a wonder boy." He glanced at Connelly and said meaningfully, "The question is whether you know what is at stake..."

Connelly replied in a well-oiled manner, "I do, Sir. I witnessed *The Cosmic Fall* four weeks ago. I was the first on site. It has become my life's mission to investigate this event in order to protect my fellow citizens and my country. I will do anything in my power to achieve this."

The High Inspector clearly wasn't impressed. "Agent Connelly, you are well aware that tensions between China and the US remain high. The US is accusing China of shooting down one of its communication satellites, while China holds the US accountable for secretly spying on them. Canada, on the other hand, is maintaining its story that the satellite was accidentally destroyed by a passing meteor, which then broke into two pieces, both of which crashed on the outskirts of Chilliwack on the night of August 26. As you know, we have been feeding this story to the news media for weeks."

He let his fingers run down the sides of his tie. The tone of his voice became serious. "But we know better, of course. We know the true nature of *The Cosmic Fall* and the threat that it may be posing to our planet. The Canadian Minister of Defense is holding a confidential meeting of the highest order next week. Both Chinese and US military officials have been invited to the table to discuss what little we know." He bent forward on his chair again, jabbing his index finger at Connelly. "*You* will be briefing this meeting."

After pausing for effect, he continued. "The fact that you witnessed *The Cosmic Fall* and that you hold a US passport through your mother has acted in your favor. The FBI has endorsed you. Inspector James Hao, here, also has dual citizenship. He was born on mainland China and is highly regarded by the Chinese Ministry of State Security. It is imperative that you work together. After this meeting takes place, the CSIS will no longer be the only Agency watching you like hawks. Do you understand?"

Connelly confirmed, "Yes, Sir."

The High Inspector straightened the files on his desk. "Your file is impeccable..." he said, before adding slowly, "Except for one thing..."

Connelly's mouth twitched.

The High Inspector removed a folder from Connelly's thick file.

"Your wife..." the High Inspector began, as he slid the folder across the desk.

Connelly took the folder and opened it. Clipped to the left side was a photograph of a smiling young woman. She had curly hair around a youthful, dark-skinned face. Her eyes were grey and her teeth a perfect white. She looked like someone straight out of a magazine. The name on the descriptive form on the right side of the folder read Tamara Connelly.

Ignoring Connelly's discomfort, the High Inspector proceeded. "You haven't returned home once since *The Cosmic Fall*. I'm not a marriage counsellor, Agent Connelly, but we've had countless calls from your wife since you arrived. She's starting to think that you abandoned her and your kid. She's threatening to take you to court to divorce you and demand full custody of your son. You say you have become obsessed with *The*

Cosmic Fall, but we can't afford to have a civilian court nosing into your business here. So either you quietly make amends with her or the next time you're in my office you'll be signing divorce papers. Either way is fine, but keep her out of the loop!"

He leaned back into his office chair, observing the Chilliwack police officer. "Any comments, Agent Connelly?"

Connelly held the High Inspector's gaze before replying through gritted teeth, "Tell me where to sign."

Taken slightly aback, the High Inspector stared at the bald man. Then he broke into a loud guffaw, his belly shaking under his impeccable suit. A palpable weight lifted in the room. The High Inspector wagged a finger at Connelly. "I like you!" he chuckled. "Forget the wife, Theodore. You're married to the job now." They were suddenly on first-name terms.

James Hao joined in. "Good thing you're getting a raise, Connelly. Child support is brutal!"

In no time, Connelly was given the necessary clearances to enter what was known as the Dugout. James Hao drove him to a plain, concrete building surrounded by lonely hills. They scanned their badges at the entrance and signed a form that a soldier handed over as he scrutinized them. They took an impressive steel elevator down seven floors. When the elevator stopped, the doors remained closed.

Hao studied Connelly intensely. "Behind these doors lies the truth of *The Cosmic Fall*. Once you walk through, there is no turning back. Do you understand?"

Connelly nodded impatiently.

Hao scanned his badge once more so the elevator doors could slide open, revealing a cavernous hangar made of concrete. Connelly stepped through onto a corridor overlooking this huge space where men and women, most wearing white coats, bustled around, working at desks full of computer screens or entering offices with glass walls bordering the left side of the hall. In the very centre, a sleek, unusual-looking craft hovered silently a few feet above the ground.

"This," Hao said dramatically, "is the intact alien spaceship we recovered from the Chilliwack crash site."

After giving Connelly a minute to take in the extraterrestrial vessel, they headed down concrete stairs to the floor of the hangar. As they circled the spacecraft, Hao explained, "We have not been able to access the vessel so far. We are using an electron beam to bore a hole into it, yet its material is so consistent that we have only been able to dent it two points of an inch. It's going to take time before we get any real results. But mark my words, we will get in eventually."

Connelly's mouth twitched. He examined the closed hangar.

Hao smiled proudly. "Impressive, isn't it?" he asked. "The craft was flown in from Chilliwack. It happened on the night of *The Cosmic Fall* under citizens' very noses. We were lucky your local police contacted the CSIS immediately. We sent in a heavyweight helicopter to pull it out in the dark before the media arrived. Then we loaded it onto a cargo aircraft Boeing C-17 and flew it over. The next feat was to lower it into this old underground bunker before building several floors above it to seal it in. We have no idea how this vessel works or what's inside, so we had to make sure it couldn't fly away on its own through some sort of remote command." Hao continued, "Bringing over the other two spacecraft was trickier, though, since they had broken into several pieces. You will be able to examine them later."

As he spoke, he gestured for Connelly to follow him down another set of stairs to the eighth and last floor. "As you know, we completed the cover-up by inserting meteor debris from Nunavut into the Chilliwack crash site to show to the media. No one was the wiser. One of the CSIS' finest moments, if you ask me."

Hao passed protective clothing and a helmet to Connelly. When they were both fully covered, he led the way into a cold, high-security chamber where three incubators lay side by side.

"And here, we have the spacecrafts' occupants," Hao breathed, as they stared at the three beings who lay in the incubators. Hao spoke in awe. "We recovered these extraterrestrials from the crash site. As you can see, they could easily pass as humans, though they are slightly taller than us. They have strong features, olive-coloured skin and high cheekbones. Their most unusual feature is their white hair. The one furthest from us is a female specimen with long, straight hair and faerie-like features. Next to her is a male of about the same age with short hair. The third being is an older male who may have been their leader."

Hao stared at Connelly to check his reaction, but he seemed unmoved by the fact that he was in the presence of creatures from outer space.

A man in a lab coat appeared behind a tall window. He gestured to Hao that he wanted to speak to him.

Nodding, he said, "I'll give you a minute to get to know our three prime 'suspects'. Too bad none of them are alive to tell us their story. Right?" He clapped Connelly on the back as he walked away.

Stiff and silent, Connelly towered over the incubators. All of a sudden his brow creased above his determined eyes and he gritted his teeth. He leaned onto the incubator closest to him with both hands and bent his head in pain. The muscles at the back of his neck twitched. Something odd was happening to his face, for it began to tremble abnormally fast behind the helmet, as if his skin had turned into rippling water.

His eyes went from green to honey-brown, his nose shrank, his face lengthened and, out of his bald head, white, spikey hair appeared. When the transformation was complete, Connelly had been replaced by an entirely different being.

He glared intensely at the lifeless aliens. Then, in the reflection of a windowpane, he noticed Hao taking leave of the man in the doctor's coat. Hao would be joining him again in no time. The being's jaw clenched in concentration. His face trembled again, his breath coming in fast gasps and sweat pearling his front.

It took all of his willpower to regain his former aspect, yet by the time Hao joined him by the incubators, Connelly's head was bald and his eyes were green again.

* * *

The family doctor blamed Ben's panic attack on his slow recovery from his illness and recommended resting for another couple of days. Ben didn't think resting would magically rid him of his nightmares and panic attacks, but Laura reminded him they had no choice but to follow the doctor's advice. After all, how was the doctor supposed to provide Ben with a decent treatment if they had not revealed the real trigger of the boy's illness?

"We can't tell the doctor the whole truth, Ben," Laura said gently, as she tucked him under a blanket on the couch. Tike lay down next to him contentedly.

Ben toyed with the TV control, pursing his lips.

"You do understand why, don't you?" Laura insisted. She brushed his fringe away with her hand.

Ben sighed.

I do.

He went over the reasons in his mind: his mother had found him unconscious, lying between the roots of a tree on the outskirts of Chilliwack, his hair covered in dirt and pieces of corn leaves, his face black with soot. By the time they had made it out of Chilliwack, military helicopters were crisscrossing the sky and reporters were flocking in to cover *The Cosmic Fall.* A heavy plume of smoke billowed off the hillside next to Grampa's house...

Laura interrupted his thoughts. "If the doctor discovers you were in Chilliwack that night, we'll find a herd of reporters and investigators swarming our apartment. I need you to recover your health, but that won't happen if there are cameras stuck to your face."

Ben groaned. "I know, I know, Mom. You told me before. I don't really care about the reporters. It's Grampa I'm worried about."

Laura knelt beside him. "I'm worried, too, honey," she said softly.

Ben asked, "Did you call him today?"

Laura looked down at her hands. "I call his house every day, Ben. I've called him a hundred times since *The Fall...*" She broke off.

Ben swallowed. "...and, still no answer?"

Laura's brows creased as she shook her head. "Still no answer."

* * *

By the next week, Ben headed back to school, but it wasn't long before he got himself noticed again, because Tike had somehow managed to escape the apartment and was found sitting politely in front of the school entrance. After the Principal realized that suspending Ben would not have any effect on the dog, and after most of the students voiced their excitement at having a cute dog "guard" their school, he decided to turn a blind eye on the problem.

From then on, Tike always accompanied Ben and waited for him patiently by the school entrance. Ben found this to be a huge relief. Knowing that his faithful friend was close-by brought him a sense of calm, and he was able to concentrate on his lessons again.

Unfortunately, the sympathy that Tike received from the students did not rub off on Ben, for he never felt the need to hang around with boys and girls from his class to talk about which movie they were going to see that weekend, or how to best handle Mr. Taylor's Math assignment.

When the school bell rang, Ben left in a hurry, hiding his dark brown eyes under his side fringe, hugging the brick wall of the school building, then crossing into a side street which fewer students used. He was barely across the road when he noticed two older boys hanging around behind a van. He swore under his breath for not having noticed them sooner, but it was too late. One of them, the tallest, shouted, "Hey! Oddball! Where ya goin'?"

Ben knew the bully's name was Peter. He hunched over, quickening his pace, but Peter called again, "Hey, wait up, Oddball. You have to meet my new friend, Mason."

Mason yelled in a sing-song voice, "Hi, Oddball!" Both boys sniggered as they followed him down the road.

Ben took off, his new backpack bouncing against his side, Tike following close behind. He was passing a chain link fence when, out of the corner of his eye, dark shadows approached him. He jumped and found three fierce-looking dogs cross a small yard to examine him up close. Ben's hair prickled at the back of his neck as the huge animals shadowed him from behind the fence. He was so mesmerized by the silent creatures that a car almost hit him as it emerged from the parking lot of an adjacent building. The man honked angrily, blocking Ben's passage.

Ben turned to face the bullies. They were just about to catch up with him when the three beasts threw themselves at the fence, barking wildly and growling menacingly. The two boys yelled, backing away in fright.

Ben stared at the scene in amazement while Tike tugged at his trouser leg as if telling him to get moving. Ben didn't need convincing. He sprinted off, heading into busier streets where he caught a bus to the coast.

* * *

Stanley Park was considered one of the most beautiful city parks in the world, nestled on a semi-island surrounded by Vancouver Harbour and English Bay. It was covered in lush, dark-green western red cedars, bigleaf maples and Douglas firs, while circled by the coveted Seawall where city dwellers and tourists alike could hike, jog, stroll, cycle or rollerblade while they enjoyed the view of the city skyline and the North Shore Mountains.

For Ben, it meant freedom to roam along forest trails or the beach while throwing a stick for

Tike to fetch. When both boy and dog had had enough, they sat on boulders in front of the Seawall, close to the empty outdoor pool, which only functioned in the summer months.

The mid-autumn afternoon ticked by. Ben's backpack lay dumped aside, forgotten, as he threw pebbles into the water. Tike tilted his head at the sight of a small crab skittering among the rocks.

"Hey, you! Kid!" someone yelled. Ben whirled, startled. A young man on a bicycle wearing high-tech cycling garments and unplugging headphones from his ears, nodded. "Yes, you!" Then he pointed towards the parking lot behind the swimming pool. "Is that your Mom?"

A car honked and several pedestrians turned disapprovingly to see who could be making such a racket. A woman waved her arm energetically through the window of the car, which Ben recognized as being his Mom's old Toyota.

"Yes, thank you," he told the cyclist, flustered. He picked up his backpack, then jogged to the car with his head down. He had barely slid into the passenger seat before she scolded him. "What's the matter with you? I've been waiting for you all afternoon! You can't go off on your own like that! What if you'd had another panic attack?"

"Mom! I'm fine!" Ben retorted. "You don't need to be on my back all the time!" He braced himself for her answer while he put on his seat belt. He was reminded of how they had always been bickering at one another before his illness. They were both stubborn that way. But this time his mother remained silent.

Ben was startled to see Laura's chin quiver as a tear rolled down her cheek. She bowed her head to let her loose hair fall to the side of her face like a curtain so he couldn't see her cry. Her breath came in short gasps, accompanied by a wheezing sound.

Asthma attack!

The anger left Ben as soon as he recognized the sound. He reached for the asthma inhaler in her handbag and gave it to her. After she had sucked in a few breaths from the medication dispenser and regained control of her breathing, he asked carefully, "Mom, what's wrong?"

She stared out the front windshield, then turned toward him. Her red-rimmed green eyes revealed that she had been crying for some time. "It's your Grampa," she said softly. "He's in the hospital."

CHAPTER 3 *Evidence*

Inspector James Hao grabbed the doorknob, then pushed the heavy wooden door into the elegant meeting room. He allowed High Inspector George Tremblay and Agent Theodore Connelly to enter first, before following them without delay. He absorbed the room's occupants with a sweeping glance: a dozen men and one woman in business suits sat around a smooth, grey-tinted table. He spotted a couple of men in military uniforms heavily covered with war decorations, while High Inspector shook hands with the woman as he made his way to the head of the table, where he invited everyone to sit down. Hao joined him, while Connelly placed himself in the shadows, close to the wall.

The High Inspector thanked everyone for making it to the emergency meeting on such short notice. "The Canadian Government," he explained, "has opted to bring China and the US to the table to discuss the true nature of *The Cosmic Fall*. The reason for this, is that the event has become an international problem. The Government is considering involving other countries but does not want to risk a breach of information to the media at this point. We will now proceed without further delay." He presented Inspector James Hao, who moved forward to take his place in front of the curious onlookers.

Hao cleared his throat, thanked the High Inspector, and began. "On August 26 at approximately 10:46 p.m., a US satellite was destroyed while in full orbit around the Earth. Less than a minute later, several witnesses on the ground reported seeing an object hurtling across the sky. It crashed on the outskirts of Chilliwack in the province of British Columbia. At 10:57 p.m., a second mass fell from the sky and exploded sixty feet from the first. You are already aware of these facts, which were reported by the media. What you do not know is that at approximately 11:23 p.m., a third object reached the same location. This one, however, did not crash." He paused for effect. "It landed." He checked his audience for their reaction and got a lot of confused stares.

The Inspector clicked the button of a remote control, triggering a projector to cast images on a blank screen behind him. A close-up of the alien spaceship appeared. He heard gasps of surprise.

"The three objects which arrived on Canadian territory on August 26 were not meteor debris, as we have led the media to believe. They were unidentified flying objects—UFOs," Hao stated. "This image is of the third spacecraft, which did not explode and which we recovered on location. It is intact but has so far proven impenetrable."

Those around the table erupted into loud talking. The High Inspector stood to silence the attendees.

Several other, less obvious pieces appeared on the screen, as Hao raised his voice over the buzz. "These are the remains of the other two vessels which exploded upon impact. After closer examination, they clearly comprise the same kind of spacecraft." The pieces on the screen danced around each other before latching together like the pieces of a three-dimensional puzzle.

Hao clicked on the remote control and the screen went blank. When an image of the three alien pilots appeared, the audience exclaimed loudly. Hao almost had to shout to make himself heard. "We recovered the remains of these three beings from the crash site." He stared seriously at the people seated before him. "As far as we know, you are looking at the first extraterrestrial visitors to Earth known to Humankind."

It took much longer, this time, for the room to quiet down. Some faces flushed with anger, others became pale and drawn, while some attendees flung a series of questions across the room. The High Inspector, Hao and Connelly waited for the excitement to die down.

"Please," the High Inspector said. "We wish to present the facts to you before taking questions." He invited Connelly to come forward. "This is Agent Theodore Connelly, a police officer from Chilliwack, currently working for the CSIS. He was the first officer on the site of the crash. He has studied the evidence and has come up with some disturbing conclusions."

As if he were giving a lecture on some tedious subject matter, Connelly began, "Three ships. Three aliens." He pointed to an image of the ships and their occupants. "We assumed there was one alien per spacecraft. However, recent evidence shows this may not be so. As you can see, there is enough room inside the vessels for several more occupants. In vessel number one, which was the first to crash, we recovered DNA from the young alien man in this area of the ship." Connelly indicated. "But we recently discovered a different, unknown DNA—here." He pointed next to the image of the young alien male, who had been placed virtually within the spacecraft.

The room went deathly quiet as the attendees digested this piece of news. One man wiped the sweat off his forehead with a cotton tissue.

The woman with graying hair and stark composure spoke the words they all were thinking. "Agent Connelly, are you telling us that we are missing an alien suspect? Possibly a live, alien suspect?"

For a second Connelly held his breath, then said clearly, "I am, Minister. One, or more than one, alien suspects, who could be halfway across the world by now."

* * *

Inspector James Hao leaned back in his office chair, a cold, wet towel pressed against his eyes. He heard his office door open and peeked under the towel to watch Connelly enter the room and throw a file on his desk. The bald man sat heavily in the chair opposite Hao.

"Do we have to do this now?" Hao grumbled, as he massaged his temples. "We just left the meeting!"

"We do," Connelly confirmed matter-of-factly.

Hao sighed. "This had better be good, wonder boy."

"It is. This is new evidence."

"What?" Hao exclaimed, the towel falling from his eyes.

"Our meeting attendees got more than they bargained for, so I opted to leave out this piece of information."

Hao frowned in disapproval but said nothing as he opened the file. A photograph of four broken pieces of glass lay before him. "What's this?"

"This evidence came from the crash site," Connelly explained. "When you assemble these pieces, they form a lens. I believe it is from a telescope."

Hao frowned, his interest piqued. "Telescope... telescope..." he mumbled. Then his eyes brightened and he got up to search through a box on the floor labelled WITNESSES. He went through several files before fishing one out. He flipped the file RYAN ARCHER on his desk. "Yeah," he said slowly, as he scanned the notes inside. "This witness stated he was stargazing in a field near his house when *The Cosmic Fall* occurred. Must be from his telescope." He shrugged as he closed the file. "Makes sense."

"But it doesn't," Connelly corrected, piercing Hao with his green eyes. He removed another picture from the file he had brought. This time it was a close-up of the lens. There were distinct fingerprints all over it. "I had these fingerprints analyzed," he explained. "Most belong to the witness, Ryan Archer. But these smaller ones didn't come up with a match."

Hao straightened in his chair to analyze the information. Slowly, he said, "Are you telling me that we have a missing witness?"

Connelly nodded. "Ryan Archer wasn't alone on the night of *The Cosmic Fall*."

"...and he failed to mention it," Hao finished, a million thoughts crossing his mind. "One missing alien. One missing witness," he began slowly. "I don't believe in coincidences. Get a team together and find out who was with Ryan Archer that night!"

He watched as Connelly picked up the file and stood with a smug smile. Just before turning to leave the office, Hao thought the Agent's eyes flickered to honey-brown. He raised an eyebrow, then shook his head. "Trick of the light," he thought, as he placed the wet towel over his face again.

* * *

By the time Ben and Laura reached Highway 1 Eastbound, it was after five o'clock, which meant they were stuck in rush hour. Ben fell asleep as the sun set behind them in a myriad of yellow and orange streaks, while Laura navigated from one busy lane to another. They had travelled half the distance to Chilliwack when Ben woke up. He stared at the cloudy night, his mind wandering. A sudden thought crossed his mind.

"Mom?" he began, irritated by his own trembling voice. "Are we staying at Grampa's house?"

Laura glanced at him. "If we can't stay at the hospital, then yes, of course we'll stay at the house."

"Really?"

Laura sighed. "I can't afford to go to a hotel,

Ben, you know that. And even if I could, I wouldn't. There's more than enough room at Grampa's house." He shot her an angry glance, so she added, "It's still our family home! What happened in the fields next to it doesn't change that."

Ben slumped back, scowling.

Laura's eyes softened. "You love that house, Ben. You remember that, don't you?"

He shrugged, saying nothing.

Yes, of course I remember. But that was before...

"You know, you're going to have to talk to Grampa." Laura interrupted his thoughts. Ben pretended to ignore her. She continued in a tender voice, "He's in intensive care, honey. He had a pretty big heart attack; he couldn't even remember his name. The nurse said the only thing they found on him was my cellphone number, which is how they got hold of me." Her voice wavered. "The thing is, I'm not sure how long he's got... You and he need to have a serious talk about what happened on the night you disappeared." She paused for a moment. "I need to have serious talk with him."

Ben turned to her, showing interest in the conversation for the first time. "Are you still angry with him?"

Laura fell silent for a moment, then replied, "Grampa has always been there for us when we've needed him. I was so proud of him for helping us out after your Dad died. Remember when I told Grampa you had the measles when you were four years old? He jumped on the first bus over! And every time a school break started, you couldn't wait for me to drive you to Chilliwack! You were having so much fun with him over the summer holidays! I could tell from our phone calls!"

She broke off, then chose her words carefully. "But what happened on the night of *The Fall* is beyond me! Why did Grampa abandon you? What were you doing miles away from the house? How did you get there? And where has Grampa been all this time? All I got from him was a single phone call in the early morning after *The Fall* letting me know that he was fine but urging me to come and pick you up in Chilliwack. Since then, not a word to find out how you were doing, or to let us know where he's been. If Tike hadn't found me that day and led me to that tree you were lying under, who knows what could have happened!" She stopped herself as she shifted in her seat. "So, yes, I am still angry!"

Ben read his mother's face like an open

book.

Not to mention out-of-your-mind with worry!

Ben turned his attention to the starry sky, mulling over what she had said, wondering whether, he, too, was angry. But he found he had a hard time grasping the feelings he had for his grandfather. Although he had excellent memories with his Grampa, his feelings for him tended to become entangled with the murky nightmare he kept having. And that was not something he wanted to linger on.

* * *

Over an hour and a half later, Ben followed his mother into the Chilliwack General Hospital with a heavy heart. He barely listened as a nurse explained that Ryan Archer was in a stable condition, and had been resting all afternoon in the Coronary Care Unit. However, he was not out of danger yet, she said. She also mentioned something about filling in some forms at the reception desk, as they were missing key information on their patient. But that could wait until later. First, she would take them to see Grampa.

Finally!

Ben saw Laura nod through the whole thing, though she seemed too shook up to reply.

When they entered Grampa's room, Laura placed a hand on Ben's shoulder to guide him to the hospital bed. Ben wasn't sure it was a gesture of comfort, rather, he guessed she needed someone to lean on, just as much as he did. And he understood why, because as soon as he saw his beloved Grampa, he had to swallow a huge lump in his throat.

Grampa was barely recognizable, tucked away in a hospital bed under crisp white sheets, his face covered by an oxygen mask, his chest hooked up to an intravenous pump and a heart monitor, beeping at the rhythm of his heart. Ben's vivid memory of a robust man, who stood tall as an oak, collided with the frail form that lay before him, and for an instant he thought they were facing the wrong patient. The old man's fading ash-blonde hair had almost turned completely white, while an unkempt beard dotted his chin.

Grampa wouldn't allow this!

Ben knew how much his Grampa railed against men who wore short stubbles, which, he declared, were neither clean shaven nor proper beards. Such laziness would not do, and he made a point to meticulously shave and comb his hair every morning. Ben held his breath as he remembered how his Grampa would affectionately attempt to paste down the lock of hair that always stuck out the back of his head.

Laura placed her hand on top of Grampa's. Ben fought against his tears as he noticed the bones under the long, thin fingers.

"Daddy?" his mother whispered.

There was no response.

They stayed beside Grampa for several hours, both crying silently, yet neither able to express their sadness.

When another nurse came by to check on Grampa, she told them they were welcome to spend the night in the waiting room. Or if they preferred, they could go home and rest: the hospital would call them if Grampa's condition changed.

Laura gave Ben a concerned glance. He took it he didn't look too great—and he didn't feel it, either.

"I'm going to fill in the forms at the reception desk," she said. "Why don't you get us something from the cafeteria? Then we'll head over to Grampa's house."

"But..." Ben objected.

"We can't leave Tike outside the hospital all night, Ben. He'll be safer at the house. There isn't much we can do right now, anyway." She spoke without much conviction.

Ben knew she wanted to stay, but decided against it for his sake. Yet he was too exhausted to argue, and the idea of his four-legged friend waiting outside the hospital was enough to make him agree.

Ben scouted for something to eat. The cafeteria had closed, so he settled for two rather dry-looking cheese sandwiches from a vending machine. He wrinkled his nose, but fed the coins into the machine anyway.

After getting the nurse to promise again that she would call if Grampa's situation changed, Laura and Ben headed to the house, which lay twenty minutes away on the outskirts of Chilliwack, surrounded by corn fields. It was almost two o'clock in the morning. The house loomed under a cloudy sky without a moon or star in sight.

Ben cowered in the car while his mother stood before the front door, illuminated by the headlights, searching for the keys in her handbag. She entered, switching on the corridor lights that splashed into the driveway. Ben reluctantly picked up their suitcases, dragging his feet inside, as Tike followed closely with his ears back and his tail between his legs.

They headed straight upstairs to the two guest rooms they had always occupied when they had vacationed at the house. Laura checked on Ben to make sure he had a warm quilt on his bed.

"Do you think Grampa will be okay?" Ben whispered from under the covers.

"I'm sure he'll be fine," she replied, before pecking his forehead to bid him goodnight. He could not read his mother's face in the dim light.

Ben closed his eyes as soon as she was gone, but his grandfather's face haunted him. He rolled around in bed and stared at the high ceiling. The room was a decent size. Grampa had painted the walls a soft blue after his grandson's birth. Two large windows looked out over the fields. An old carpet, a sturdy bed next to a nightstand, a cupboard with three drawers displaying a couple of photographs of baby Ben and Grampa, a sofa and several shelves with wooden toys and books Ben had played with for as long as he could remember filled the familiar room.

Ben was about to close his eyes again when something caught his attention. He sat, suddenly alert. On a shelf on the opposite wall perched a sleek, white telescope. He had never seen it before. He got out of bed, pushed the sofa closer to the wall and clambered onto it before carefully removing the beautiful object. It still had the store tag attached to it.

It's brand new!

As he hopped off the sofa, something clanked inside it. He unwound the lens, then tilted the telescope to release the item that had come loose.

A silver watch slipped into his lap, followed by a piece of paper.

Ben stared at the unexpected items, then unfolded the note. It read, "Dear Ben, I believe this jewel is yours. I found it under the kitchen sink. Remember me when you look at the stars. Love, Grampa."

Ben stared at the note, then at the watch. At the centre of it glimmered a beautiful gem that might have been a diamond, though he didn't think diamonds shone this much. He wondered if Grampa had had it placed in the watch on purpose. One thing was certain, he had no recollection of it.

He sat on the edge of the bed for a long moment, sniffing and wiping his eyes with the back of his shirt as he stared at the items. When exhaustion gained on him, he let himself sink into bed. He covered his head with the bed sheets and fell into a deep sleep, the watch clasped tightly in his hand.

* * *

Tike lay next to a sleeping Ben, when a movement caught his attention. The dog lifted his head, his ears upright.

A tall man with white, wavy hair stood in the bedroom beside one of the windows. Tike sniffed the air and stared at the strange man from a few feet away. Then the form turned his head, distracted by something happening outside.

Tike jumped off the bed and stood on his hind legs to peek out the other window. Deer had materialized onto the fields, their antlers rising proudly over the cold mist. The animals remained in front of the house for a long time.

Then, as suddenly as he had appeared, the white-haired man vanished, leaving Tike staring curiously at the room.

* * *

In a bright, white office on the third floor of

the Dugout, a CSIS fax machine clicked on, releasing a sheet of paper. A police report appeared bearing a picture of Ryan Archer's face. A red, handwritten note read, "Location: Chilliwack General Hospital."

CHAPTER 4 *Tiwanaku*

A tall man sat on the large steps of the Kalasasaya temple—an ancient monument that belonged to the ruins of Tiwanaku, a city built many centuries ago by pre-Inca people of South America. A cold breeze blew through the visitor's white, wavy hair, as he gazed at a stunning sunrise over the dry Andes mountain range which crossed eastern Bolivia. Behind him towered an impressive door built of perfectly carved stones, leading to an open courtyard guarded by a ten-foot monolith representing some forgotten deity.

In spite of his unusual hair, the man's strong features belonged to someone in his mid-thirties. He wore a crimson poncho over his long-sleeved shirt, protecting him from the early morning temperature. Closing his honey-coloured eyes, he let the sun warm his olive-tanned face. He did not immediately turn to greet the old Aymara native who had walked up behind him. After enjoying his fill of high altitude sunlight, the visitor stood and joined the older man, who offered him a broad smile.

"*Suma urukiya[1]*, Observer," the old Aymara greeted.

The visitor's eyes softened as he answered, "*Buenos días[2]*, Amaru."

"We have been waiting for you for a long time," Amaru said, before noticing that the visitor's attention had turned to the monolith placed centrally behind the gateway. Understanding his attraction to it, Amaru nodded. "It represents our shaman ancestor. A great shapeshifter. A rare skill, indeed, as you well know..." He trailed off.

They stared at it for a moment, before Amaru ventured, "You barely made it here alive. And yet I have been told that you wish to return to the crash site! Are you sure that is a wise decision?"

---

[1] *Suma urukiya* = 'Good day' in Aymara.

[2] *Buenos dlas* = 'Good morning' in Spanish

The visitor's gaze was lost in the distance as he replied, "Last night I had a vision. A spirit portal called me back to the crash site. Only one of my own could have sent me such a powerful message. It has to be my daughter! I must return to find out if she is still alive!"

Amaru sized up the white-haired stranger, before sighing and reaching inside his poncho. He produced a dark blue Canadian passport which he presented to the tall man. The stranger flipped through the pages until he found the identity and photograph of the passport's original owner. The name read Jack Anderson from Ottawa, Ontario. The face of a young man stared back at him with determination.

"Our scouts found Jack Anderson's body along the Inca Trail," Amaru explained. "He was reported missing two days ago after he went trekking on his own. Our scouts found his remains at the bottom of the mountainside. We have not yet informed authorities that we have found him. Therefore, his passport will serve you for the next twenty-four hours. That is enough to get you back to Canada. But by tomorrow afternoon, we will be returning this poor man's body to his family."

The visitor nodded. "Yes, of course. I understand." He stared at Amaru, then said with sincerity, "*Gracias*[3], Amaru."

Amaru dismissed his thanks, continuing, "With luck, you will pass as Jack Anderson when you reach airport security." The old man dug into his poncho again and pulled out a beige fur hat with ear flaps so that the visitor could cover his unnaturally white hair. "Let us hope that this will do."

The visitor stared at his Aymara friend, sensing that he was not happy with the situation. "Amaru, my friend, rest assured that when the time comes, I will speak a good word for you."

Amaru glanced away hastily, clearly uncomfortable with the visitor's words.

"What is it?" the white-haired man asked, frowning.

Taking courage, Amaru said, "You are the Observer. Your mission is to be neutral and report the facts." He paused. "But dark forces are at work. Your companions have perished. Your daughter is lost, and you barely survived yourself. We fear that you are no longer neutral, that your judgment has been clouded."

The visitor put up a hand. "You said 'we'..."

Amaru stared at him unhappily, knowing

---

[3] *Gracias* = 'Thank you' in Spanish.

that he had to finish now that he had started speaking his mind. "Yes. I speak for all the Wise Ones." He paused before adding carefully, "We have given you the information you came for, as is customary. It is not our place to judge. But word is spreading that you have already made up your mind about your mission. The word is that your loss has blinded you."

The visitor replied sternly, "You cannot know my mind. I have made no decision, and I have yet to meet two Wise Ones."

Amaru bowed respectfully. "We understand. There is time yet." He led the visitor down the perfectly polished steps of the temple, away from a group of tourists who had appeared on the archeological site. "No matter," he continued. "What I meant to say is that I do not need you to put in a good word for me. I do not wish to leave this place. I have a wife, many children and grandchildren. We have wood for the fire, our llamas for warm fur and the most beautiful sunrises and sunsets on this planet. We could ask for nothing more."

The tall visitor stared at the old man in disbelief as they walked along the temple walls. After a long silence, he placed a firm hand on Amaru's shoulder, saying, "Perhaps you are wiser than the wisest, Amaru. Thank you for speaking your mind. I do not understand your wish, but I will respect it. When the time comes, rest assured that your name will not be mentioned. You will remain on this planet." He paused, before adding explicitly, "For better or for worse."

Relief washed over Amaru's face. He offered a wide smile. "Come, then, now that that is settled, we must get you on your way."

Before them lay the Akapana pyramid, where a group of Aymara men dressed in red ponchos and colourfully knitted caps with earflaps were waiting for them. When they approached, the group of men bowed their heads, saying in greeting, "*Suma urukiya*, Mesmo."

* * *

When Ben got up the next morning, he showered hurriedly and glanced out his bedroom window while dressing. Next to his grandfather's house lay a field of browning corn crops, bordered by a line of trees and shrubs. Beyond that lay the famous field where *The Cosmic Fall* had occurred. Even though branches hampered the view, he could tell that the area was still sealed off by yellow tape to warn trespassers, though some of it had come loose and was flapping in the wind.

Higher up the hillside and overlooking part of the field, was Mr. Victor Hayward's modern, West-Coast-styled dwelling. Grampa's neighbour was a wealthy man who owned his own airline company, and this house was only one of his many different properties across the country. People in town said he was a big player in the Alberta oil sands, which meant he was away often.

Ben sighed and stroked Tike's back. He could hear his mother bustling in the kitchen, so he clambered down the stairs to join her. Tike did not follow him, preferring to sniff intently at a spot by the window.

The boy found his mother throwing out smelly items from the fridge. She had opened the kitchen door wide to let in fresh air.

"Morning, Ben. I guess we'll head out right away. The fridge and the pantry are empty. We'll find some breakfast at the hospital."

Ben nodded as he finished putting on his hoodie sweater. "I wonder where Grampa has been all this time," he said, noticing how the house had an abandoned feeling to it.

"Yes," Laura agreed, clearly unhappy and worried. "Let's hope we get some answers soon."

They argued about whether to leave Tike out in the backyard while they were at the hospital. Ben refused to leave his four-legged friend behind, but Laura convinced him that Tike would be more comfortable at the house since the hospital did not allow pets inside. Ben reluctantly agreed, then hurriedly left so he wouldn't have to look at Tike's pleading eyes.

* * *

Twenty minutes later they had reached the hospital again, where they found things unchanged. Grampa remained stable and unresponsive. They hung around in his room; Laura sat by his bed and stroked his hand, Ben read magazines and switched through TV channels without really paying much attention. Looking for a distraction, Ben ended up going down to the gift shop while Laura fell asleep on a chair in the waiting area.

No sooner had she dozed off, when a nurse touched her shoulder. "He's awake," she announced.

Laura sprang up and hurried to the room, where she found her father with his eyes open.

She rushed to his side. "Dad!"

The nurse removed his oxygen mask before checking his vital signs. "Take it easy on him," she advised before leaving.

Laura took her father's hand. "Dad? It's Laura."

Her father's eyes focused, creasing into a smile. "Honeybee..." he began, his voice frail.

Laura's chin wavered at hearing her nickname, but she pulled herself together and shushed him. "Stay calm, Daddy. You suffered a heart attack. You're at the Chilliwack General Hospital"

She saw him frown worriedly for the briefest moment. Then he closed his eyes as if needing time to accept the news. When he opened them again, he asked unexpectedly, "How come you're not angry at me?"

Laura suppressed a nervous burst of laughter. She recognized her Dad's sense of humour. "Oh, Daddy," she said with fake anger. "I'm *furious* at you!"

Ryan relaxed, forcing a small smile. "Oh, good," he breathed. "You confused me there for a minute."

Laura couldn't keep up the pretense. Her face crumpled. "I missed you so much!"

Ryan's smile faded. "Me, too, Honeybee." He

tapped her hand reassuringly. He scanned the room with his eyes. "Where's Ben?"

"He'll be up in a minute. I sent him to the gift shop to keep his mind busy. He becomes restless when Tike's not with him."

"Huh!" Ryan said weakly. "So he's still got that yapping scoundrel?"

Laura didn't answer. Instead, she said, "He's missed you, too, you know."

Ryan frowned, then responded with a twinkle in his eye, "The yapping scoundrel misses me?"

Laura smiled a watery smile. "No, silly, I meant Ben. He's missed you so much. We've been worried sick about you! I couldn't find you anywhere!" She broke off, her words caught in her throat. "Now is not the time, but when you feel up to it, we need to talk about what happened."

Ryan had become serious, the cheeky twinkle in his eye fading as he spoke. "I need to talk to you, too, Honeybee."

"Not now, Daddy. You need to get better first. The nurse said you need to rest. It can wait until you feel stronger."

Ryan shook his head and wanted to speak, but a hissing cough left his cracked lips instead. Laura helped him drink sips of water from a plastic cup. "Listen to me now," he began again. "Remember that notary on Knight Road?" When she nodded, he said, "He has my will."

Laura opened her mouth to protest, but he silenced her. "I'm leaving the house to Benjamin." Laura gaped, so he went on quickly. "No, listen! I know you don't want to live out there, but you can rent the place. You'll get good money from it. It will keep you afloat while you live in Vancouver. You will be the custodian of the house until Ben turns eighteen. Then he will decide what to do with it. He can sell it or live in it. I don't care. He will decide."

"Dad," Laura jumped in. "I had to drag Ben to the house last night. He's refused to go back in all these weeks because..." She stopped.

"...he's afraid," Ryan finished.

Laura nodded, glad they were on the same page. "He's terrified," she confirmed. She hesitated, but the burning question left her lips before she could help herself. "Why is he terrified, Dad?"

He would not meet her eyes. There was a long silence before he asked, "Do you two still fight?"

She sighed, looking away, frustrated that he was changing the subject.

Ryan pushed on. "You shouldn't take it out on him, you know, just because he has his father's looks." Laura glared at him, but Ryan continued. "He's a lot more like you than you know. All you see in him are his father's handsome face, brown hair and eyes, but inside... inside he's just like you, strong and stubborn and witty all at the same time. You should spend more time with him. He can be a lot of fun, believe me!" He let his words sink in, before adding, "I want you to take the boy on a long vacation, somewhere far away. Don't fuss about expenses! I'm leaving you a good sum of money, too."

"Dad!" she exclaimed, truly offended this time.

"Don't interrupt me, young lady!" Ryan snapped. "You get that boy away from here! And don't give me that excuse again that you have to work. You'll manage to make ends meet, I promise you. Take that boy on a trip and get to know him. He needs you!"

Laura couldn't face him. Too much anger boiled inside. She was the one who had planned on giving him a piece of her mind, yet somehow the tables had turned, and now he was the one lecturing her. "He needs you, too, you know!" she retorted. "You have no idea what we've been through! The nightmares, the long nights watching over him while he shook with fever! I had no idea how to deal with it because I had no idea what had happened! Yes, I understand that some freakish meteorite landed in your backyard and that it's a crazy thing to wrap your head around, but what was I supposed to do? How the heck was I supposed to talk to him about a thing like that?"

She was sobbing again, and it took all her willpower to whisper, "Where were you? Why didn't you call?" She barely realized he was squeezing her hand, inviting her to look at the door.

She found Ben standing there awkwardly.

Laura, caught off guard, raised her hand to her mouth. Her breath started coming in short gasps. Nervously, she reached for her handbag and took a couple of deep breaths from the asthma inhaler.

"I'm sorry," she whispered sincerely, before walking out.

* * *

Ben felt awkward being in the room alone with his grandfather, perhaps because he barely recognized the man who, not so long ago, had seemed like a sturdy oak, with his booming voice and roars of laughter. Now he was pale and thin, a shadow of who he had once been. Or perhaps it was the invisible wall of silence that had built up between them since his absence.

It was Ryan who spoke first. "I see your Mom found you okay..."

Ben knew he was referring to the day after *The Cosmic Fall*, when his mother had found him unconscious under a tree. He nodded.

Ryan's face relaxed. "Good, good," he said half to himself. The old man cleared his throat.

He's as uncomfortable as I am! Ben felt a pang of emotion at this realization.

"Are you studying hard, boy? Are you keeping up your grades?"

Ben nodded again briefly.

I don't want to talk about school grades.

Ryan repeated, "Good, good. Your mother tells me you're staying at the house?"

Once more, Ben nodded, staring down at his feet.

"Look at me, Potatohead," his Grampa ordered, using the nickname he had for his grandson. "She says you don't like it there anymore..." Since Ben continued to study the patterns on the floor, Grampa added softly, "...because of the nightmares."

This time Ben's head shot up, his eyes wide.

"Yeah..." Grampa acquiesced, before adding quietly, "I get them, too."

Ben went to stand by his grandfather's bedside. "You... you get them, too?" he asked shakily. "What do they mean? The nightmares? I can't remember anything. The doctor says I have amnesia."

Grampa studied the twelve-year-old intently. "Do you know what amnesia is, son? It's the brain's ability to protect you from disturbing memories. It keeps you sane. Have you ever thought that, perhaps, it was a good thing you have amnesia, and that, for your own sanity, it should stay that way?"

Ben stared at him, stunned. Whatever he had expected from his grandfather, this was not it. Somehow he had hoped for an explanation. He felt terribly deceived. "How can you say such a thing, Grampa? You're supposed to help me remember! So I can heal!"

To his bewilderment, his grandfather's lower lip began to tremble. The words came out with difficulty as he sobbed. "I'm sorry this happened to you, Ben."

"What do you mean, Grampa?" Ben asked quickly. "Sorry... *what*... happened?"

Grampa wheezed, "I'm sorry I wasn't there for you when you needed me."

Ben didn't know what his grandfather was apologizing for, but he was only too aware of the heart monitor that beeped unevenly. He took his grandfather's hand firmly. "It's okay, Grampa. It wasn't your fault."

Ryan nodded, a heavy weight visibly lifting from his heart. His hand clenched painfully around Ben's own as he gasped for air.

Two nurses appeared and rushed around the bed.

"You'll have to wait outside, son," one of them said urgently.

"Ben!" Grampa gasped. He struggled to speak now. A nurse put a firm hand on Ben's shoulder, but he shook her off. He bent down and put his ear close to Grampa's mouth.

Grampa breathed, "If... danger... find... Mesmo!"

Mesmo.

The name echoed in Ben's mind.

Ryan Archer sank into the pillows as a nurse placed the oxygen mask on his face again. Ben held onto his grandfather's hand, his eyes streaming with tears. "I love you, Grampa!" He could see Grampa's watery eyes returning the words as the nurse led him away.

Laura ran down the corridor, closely followed by a doctor who rushed into the room without saying a word, leaving them both stranded and huddling together.

‎ ◆

CHAPTER 5 *Twisted Eyes*

Ben paced the corridor, throwing sideway glances at his mother. Laura's brow creased over her empty gaze as she bit her nails. He couldn't bear to watch her anguished face, so instead he followed the hands of the clock on the wall as they ticked away the minutes.

At last, the doctor came out to tell them that Mr. Archer was stable again. From what he understood, he said, the family had not seen each other in a while, so he cautioned them not to bring up too many strong emotions at this stage. He would reevaluate the patient's health in the morning.

Ben drew a deep breath, yet felt helpless as to what to do next. Waiting and doing nothing was nerve wracking, so his mother took him for dinner at the hospital cafeteria. He wasn't hungry, but it took his mind off things for a while.

They hung around for several more hours in the waiting room, until a nurse went to check on Grampa and informed them that nothing had changed.

By then it was one o'clock in the morning. Most of the hospital was dark and the corridors empty. When Laura suggested they get some rest at the house, Ben didn't even protest. He felt like he had spent the entire day on an emotional roller-coaster. Laura put her arm around his shoulder as they slowly headed for the exit.

A bald doctor in a white coat brushed past them. Ben caught the man's honey-brown eyes briefly as he moved away to let the doctor through.

Twisted eyes...

Something unpleasant tugged at the back of Ben's mind. But the moment vanished as soon as they stepped through the hospital doors into fresh air and he remembered that Tike was waiting for him.

When they reached Grampa's house, Ben hugged his four-legged friend happily. Tike licked the boy's face and wagged his tail excitedly. As boy and dog headed upstairs, Ben realized he had left the watch Grampa had given him on his bedside table. He vowed to put it on again as soon as he went to bed.

* * *

The bald doctor in the white coat followed the directions to the Coronary Care Unit. Once there, he picked up a clipboard containing patient information that was placed on top of the reception desk, without addressing the two nurses who chatted at the far end. He saw several screens behind the desk, some showing images from cameras laid out in the hospital corridors, while others monitored patients' status. He made sure the nurses were still talking before reaching over to touch the screens, which immediately turned to static. Satisfied, the bald man headed down the corridor and entered a room.

Ryan Archer rested in the dim light, his heart beating regularly.

The doctor closed the door, then locked it.

Ryan's voice sounded frail in the silence. "Who's there?"

The doctor walked to the heart monitor, then followed the IV line from the intravenous pump to Ryan's arm with the tip of his fingers.

Ryan asked, "Why did you lock the door?"

The doctor appeared in his field of vision. He wore a grey business suit, light blue shirt and tie under the doctor's white coat as if he had attended a business meeting before coming to the hospital. He studied Ryan with emotionless eyes. "You are Mr. Archer, yes?"

Ryan rolled his eyes, resigned. "I know who you are. You all look the same with your dainty suits." He stared back at the doctor before adding, "CSIS? FBI? What do you want now? I already told your buddies everything. Can't you see I'm on my deathbed? Give a man some peace!"

The fake doctor replied coldly, "Yes, I read your witness file. Quite interesting. But many gaps. Your story may have made sense to my 'buddies'. But not to me." He sat down on the edge of Ryan's bed, saying purposefully, "You see, you forgot to mention Mesmo."

Ryan stared at him in stunned silence, a veil of fear passing before his eyes. He glanced away, but too late, the man had captured his reaction. "Who are you?" Ryan whispered strenuously, trying to hide his discomfort.

The man quoted matter-of-factly, "I am Theodore Edmond Connelly, agent with the

Canadian Security Intelligence Service..." He stopped, before adding darkly, "Though Mesmo would know me by another name." He sighed, seeming bored. "Nothing that concerns you, though."

Ryan stared at him in disgust. "What do you want?" His breath quickened behind the oxygen mask.

Connelly bent over until he was face to face with Ryan, his voice coming in a slow, intense growl. "I want Mesmo! Where is he?"

Cold sweat dampened Ryan's forehead. Something odd was happening with the fake doctor's eyes. They were switching from green to honey-brown, then back to green.

Connelly continued, "You know who I am talking about. I want Mesmo! And you're going to tell me where he is!"

Ryan gritted his teeth. "How can you know Mesmo? No-one at the CSIS knows Mesmo. You're lying! Who are you, really?"

Connelly smiled at him coldly, pleased that Ryan was coming to his own conclusions. Whereas the fake doctor had been bald a minute ago, now white, prickly hair stuck out of his head. He looked away into the distance, seeming to remember something pleasant. "Let's just say," he began, "that I am the one who made sure Mesmo's spacecraft crashed into a million pieces in your fields on the night of *The Cosmic Fall*." He turned to Ryan again, waiting for his words to sink in. His eyes became honey-brown again, and the muscle on the side of his neck twitched abnormally.

Ryan fought to keep a straight face, but his speeding heartbeat on the monitor gave him away. He understood. And he was afraid.

Connelly's smile faded. "Too bad Mesmo made it out alive. My mission would have ended all those weeks ago. Instead, I have had to endure this repulsive human face for weeks. I am tired and impatient. And when I am impatient, my anger tends to run out of control." He glared menacingly. "I am running out of patience now, Mr. Archer. Tell me where I can find Mesmo!"

Ryan whimpered. With a trembling arm, he tried to reach for the red call button on the wall behind his bed, but it was too far away.

Connelly grabbed Ryan's arm, pushing it down onto the bed. "Tell me!" he threatened.

The heart monitor beeped wildly as Ryan's breath became ragged, but his eyes hardened as he gasped. "You are a murderer! You won't get anything out of me!"

The alien put his mouth very close to Ryan's

ear, making his skin crawl. "Maybe," he snarled, "I should ask your grandson!"

* * *

That night, the nightmares returned.

Twisted eyes!

Ben woke up screaming. He opened his eyes dizzily, trying to catch his bearings. When he recognized where he was, he tumbled back into bed, breathing heavily.

In an instant, Laura rushed to his side, shushing him and rubbing his back, until drowsiness carried him away again.

The next time his eyelids flew open, it was still dark and Laura had fallen asleep by his side. He caught sight of the watch he had left under the bedside lamp and reached for it in the dark. He put it on his wrist and covered his head with the bedsheet. Holding on tightly to the watch with his other hand, he calmed down and fell into an uneasy slumber once more.

* * *

In the room, by the window, a tall man with

white, wavy hair appeared. Though his eyes were lost in the shadows, he observed the woman and Ben's form lying under the bedsheets.

He took a step forward.

The shrill sound of a phone echoed through the dark house. From somewhere in his deep slumber, Ben heard his mother gasp for air. He vaguely registered Laura leaving the bed, then heard her bare feet patter down the stairs.

The high-pitched sound persisted, finally pulling Ben from his sleep. He scanned the empty room, confused, then heard Laura's muffled voice turn to grief.

Grampa!

He sat upright in bed, fully awake.

Ben and his mother rushed to the Chilliwack General Hospital where they found a lot of commotion on Grampa's floor: hospital staff rushed around semi-dark hallways, talking intensely in low voices. They found a doctor and two nurses bathed in a ghostly, red glow from the emergency lights as they stood in the hallway before Grampa's room. The doctor broke the news: Grampa had passed away thirty minutes earlier.

Ben listened in disbelief as the doctor explained that Grampa had fallen out of bed, where the nurses had found him in cardiac arrest. Despite their best efforts, they had not been able to revive him.

Ben stepped away, his mind in turmoil, unable to conceive the news. He watched from a distance as the doctor talked quietly with his distraught mother. Then the doctor excused himself, saying that he needed to check in on his other patients because the hospital had experienced a brief outage.

One of the nurses asked Laura if she wanted to see her father one last time before they took him away.

Ben watched his mother nod.

Then, in a grief-filled voice, Laura asked, "Did he say anything, before...?" A sob stopped her from finishing the sentence.

"Well, he did, actually," The nurse replied. "But I'm afraid it didn't make much sense."

Laura waited expectantly.

"He said 'Find Mesmo.' Well, that's what I could make of it, anyway." The nurse shrugged apologetically. "Do you have any idea what that might mean?"

Laura lowered her eyes and shook her head.

Behind her, Ben's face turned ghostly pale.

* * *

The immigration officer eyed the tall man in the fur hat, then glanced at the dark blue passport he held in his hand. Before him, a crowd of tired but patient travellers chatted while waiting to be cleared through Customs and Immigration of the bustling Toronto Airport.

"What's with the hat?" the officer asked.

The man straightened the beige hat with ear flaps, so that the officer could get a better look at his face without removing it from his head. "A souvenir from South America," he explained. "From a guide who trekked with me through the Andes Mountains."

The officer eyed him without showing the slightest emotion. He checked something on his screen for an annoying amount of time, then reached for a stamp on his desk.

His phone rang. The officer picked up the receiver and listened silently. "Yes, Sir," was all he said, before hanging up. He stared at his screen thoughtfully, picked up the stamp again and pressed it onto Jack Anderson's passport, leaving a circular ink mark, allowing the man entry.

"Welcome back to Canada, Mr. Anderson," the officer said, offering the passport back to the man.

Mesmo reached out, but the officer held on to it. He pointed behind him at the different line-ups leading to baggage reclaim. "Your connecting Victory Air flight to Vancouver is the first exit to the left. You don't have much time. Your luggage will follow automatically," he explained.

Mesmo nodded. The officer let go of the passport.

The tall alien, travelling under the name Jack Anderson, headed away from the cumbersome immigration officer and let out a low sigh of relief. He strode down the large hall and noticed an exit with a paper sign that read, "Victory Air 217, Vancouver."

Mesmo plunged through the automatic doors, briefly noting that he was the only traveller heading to that destination.

Five men in business suits waited on the other side.

"It's him," one imposing man said into a tiny speaker attached to his ear, as the doors slid shut behind Mesmo.

The other four men lunged at the alien, pinning him to the ground. Swiftly, the imposing man injected something into Mesmo's neck. The alien felt his muscles go weak and his sight blurred.

"We have him, boss," the man announced quietly into the speaker, as Mesmo lost consciousness.

CHAPTER 6 *Mesmo*

Two days later, Laura and Ben stood in the rain before Grampa's grave, dressed in black raincoats covering a black dress and a dark grey suit, respectively. They had trouble concentrating on the priest's eulogy, as they were taken aback by the number of people who had shown up at the funeral.

"I placed a small announcement with the date and time of the funeral in the Chilliwack Times obituary," Laura whispered to Ben with an emotional voice. "But I hadn't expected anyone else to come."

When the ceremony was over, people streamed away after paying their respects. Ben edged away, too overcome with sadness to be able to handle a conversation with the locals, who, he remembered, had known his mother and grandparents for years.

Tike had wandered off, giving the boy an excuse to search the green graveyard. He found his dog sitting alert next to a thick tree surrounded by shrubs. Glad to have something else to think about, Ben walked over to his faithful companion to see what had caught his attention.

"Tike?" Ben called, before realizing a man was standing unmoving next to the tree. Tike gazed up at the stranger, his tail wagging uncertainly.

Ben stopped in surprise, glancing at the tall man who wore jeans, a brown jacket and a curious fur hat with ear flaps. The outfit looked utterly out of place for a funeral, yet there was something vaguely familiar about him. "Hi," Ben said timidly, encouraged by Tike's trusting attitude. The man stared at him without replying. "Er... did you know my grandfather?"

The man's face was drawn as if he had not slept in a long time or was fighting off an illness. "Yes," he replied without further explanation.

"Oh," was all Ben could say in return, noticing the stranger's unhealthy grey-tinted skin. The man gazed intently at Ben's arm. Ben lifted it up, confused, then remembered the watch that Grampa had given him. He tentatively turned his arm towards the stranger, the words slipping from his mouth. "It was my Grampa's before..." he broke off, nodding in the direction of the ceremony.

The man stared at the funeral procession, then up and down at Ben. He suddenly swayed and reached for the bark of the tree to steady himself.

"Are you okay?" Ben asked worriedly.

The man tilted his chin and winced. "Yes," he said forcefully as he straightened himself.

Ben opened his mouth to say something when Laura walked up beside him. "Oh, hello," she said to the stranger. "It's nice to see you again." Ben blinked at her in astonishment, as she continued, "I'm Laura, Ryan's daughter. Do you remember?" She held out her hand to greet him. "I'm sorry, but I don't remember your name?"

To their surprise the man stepped back, avoiding her touch by putting his hands in his pockets. Laura dropped her hand awkwardly. "Jack Anderson," the man said briefly as a manner of greeting.

Ben glared at his mother, waiting for an explanation.

"I met Jack a few weeks ago," she told him, her face flushed. "After you were well enough to go back to school, I drove out to Chilliwack, in the hopes your grandfather had returned from wherever it was he had disappeared to…" She waved her hand vaguely. "Instead, I found Jack here taking care of Grampa's place." She shook her head, remembering. "I never did get to see Grampa that time," she said sadly, before turning to Jack and adding, "Thank you for checking up on the house, by the way."

Jack nodded in acknowledgment. "Your father helped me through some difficult times."

"He seems to have helped a lot of people," she agreed, pointing to the dwindling crowd. Two elderly ladies under an umbrella waved her over. "Oh, I have to go," she said, sounding disappointed. "Er… why don't you come over to the house later? It looks like we're having an unplanned reception. We can talk further there, away from the rain."

When Jack didn't answer, Laura waved at him shyly before heading over to the two women who wanted to pay their respects.

Ben stared at Jack with new curiosity. "Will you come? To the house, I mean?" he was eager to talk to someone who had seen his grandfather in the past weeks.

The man shook his head. "I came here hoping to find someone." He gazed intensely at Ben, then added slowly, "But now I know I won't find her here." He took a deep breath, then turned around, saying, "Goodbye, Benjamin."

How do you know my name?

Ben felt an urge to hold the man back. "Wait!" he blurted. "Have we met before?"

Jack glanced back before replying, "Yes." When he saw Ben staring at him hopefully, he added, "Your grandfather told me you couldn't remember." He paused. "It's probably better that way." He turned around again and strode off.

"That's what Grampa said!" Ben called after him. "That it was best I didn't remember. But I want to remember!"

Still, Jack kept on walking.

Ben's heart thumped desperately. He felt a pull towards this stranger. A small lock of white hair sticking out from under the fur hat triggered something in his mind.

Mesmo.

"Mesmo!" Ben yelled.

The man froze in his tracks, then slowly turned. Man and boy stared at each other.

"Grampa told me, just before he died, to find

Mesmo," Ben said in awe. "You're Mesmo!"

I know it!

Though the man's eyes softened, he replied sadly, "I'm sorry, Benjamin. I can't help you." This time he didn't stop walking as he disappeared into the trees.

"Wait!" Ben ran after him. The branches swayed gently in the wind while the rain pattered on the yellowing leaves. Mesmo was gone. Ben and Tike found themselves at the edge of the forest, alone. Ben gazed back towards Grampa's grave; his eyes filled with tears.

His mom waited for him by the car. She opened the door as he trudged sadly over to her. Silently, they headed back to the house, leaving the soggy graveyard behind.

* * *

Not far off, a plume of smoke came out of the exhaust pipe of a white, unmarked van. Inside, two men in business suits typed on computer keyboards as they spoke through headsets. Inspector James Hao hovered behind them, surveilling the information on the various screens as he sipped on a cup of coffee. One of the men pulled up photographs of the funeral so he could review them.

"Send this off for processing immediately. I want a name for every face on these pictures," Hao ordered.

Fifteen minutes later, the van door slid open, and Connelly appeared in the rain behind them. He climbed in and pulled the door closed before taking off his dripping coat.

Hao cornered him, hissing, "Agent Connelly. You missed the whole thing! Where have you been?"

Connelly held his gaze before replying coldly, "Investigating."

Hao retorted in a menacing low voice, "You may have impressed the big guys at the Dugout, wonder boy! But remember who's in charge here! You do not go off on your own without prior authorization. I want a report on your current investigations on my desk by tomorrow. Do you understand?"

Connelly's mouth twitched, and it was only after a pause that bordered on insubordination, that he answered, "Yes, Sir."

Hao backed away, satisfied. "Good!" He grabbed his coat before opening the van door. "I'll take over from here." He shut the door with a bang, walked to a silver Nissan and slid inside. He drove off, the white van following closely.

* * *

It didn't take long for the house to fill up
with people from Chilliwack. Laura suspected
they had called each other, agreeing to meet. She
didn't even have to worry about food or drinks;
they appeared magically in the kitchen and living
room with every person that arrived. She felt
overwhelmed by so much attention. One person
after another told her about how Grampa had
helped them in one way or another. She even
found herself talking for several minutes with a
man in ragged clothes, long, unkempt beard, and
weird knitted beanie hat. She suspected he was a
homeless man everyone in Chilliwack referred to
as Wayne the Bagman because he always trudged
around town with his few possessions packed in a
garbage bag. Laura wouldn't have been surprised
if her Dad had met him while helping at the local
shelter.

People lined up to talk to her. They wanted
to tell her their stories of how they remembered
Laura as a small girl or how her sick mother had
passed away prematurely. Naturally, the
conversation always tended to switch to *The*

Cosmic Fall, and how the fallen meteors had affected every Chilliwack resident in one way or another.

From the corner of her eye, Laura caught Ben sneaking between people's backs, a ham sandwich in his mouth. She excused herself from a woman who asked her where her father had been the past six weeks. She took Ben by the arm, pulling him away until they found themselves in the large pantry next to the kitchen. She shut the door, switched on the light and leaned back.

She stood there for a moment, her ears ringing from so much chatter, staring at Ben in disbelief. They both burst into a nervous giggle.

"Who *are* all these people?" Ben asked, wide-eyed.

"I think half of Chilliwack is here! Grampa was some Chilliwack hero, by the looks of it," Laura said.

She stifled laughter at the thought. It felt good to release their emotions like this, even though it seemed highly inappropriate to be laughing at a funeral reception. Somehow, though, Laura knew her father would have approved.

Once the ringing in her ears had eased, Laura glanced at Ben worriedly. "How are you holding up?"

He shrugged, but answered bravely, "I'm okay."

Laura hesitated for a moment. "I spoke to Mrs. Gallagher. She and her husband run an accounting business downtown. Anyway, she's heading for Vancouver later to visit her daughter." She paused, before adding. "She has offered to take you with her. I think you should go."

"What? No way! Why? What about you?"

"I need to stay here to take care of things. I got a call from the notary in Chilliwack. He wants me to come in tomorrow for Grampa's will. I think you, on the other hand, might be better off at home. You've had nightmares ever since we got here. You were right; this place isn't doing you any good," she admitted. "Anyway, tomorrow is a school day. It might take your mind off things."

Ben groaned.

"Think about it, Ben. I'm going to be dealing with funeral companies, notaries, and bankers. You'd find yourself on your own while I dealt with this administrative mess. I'd feel better if you were back home with some routine. It might help with the nightmares."

She saw Ben open his mouth, then close it again in resignation. He nodded reluctantly.

"I'll only be a couple of days at the most,"

she said apologetically.

"It's okay, Mom," Ben said gruffly.

Laura's heart bulged. She hugged him and said. "I'm sorry you and Grampa didn't get a chance to talk."

She heard him swallow a sob as he hid his face in her sweater. She thought he was going to tell her something, but instead he said, "Can I ask you something?"

Laura stroked the side fringe out of his eyes. "Of course, honey. Anything!"

Ben spoke slowly. "Why do I have Grampa's last name? I mean, Dad's name was Robert Manfield, wasn't it? So why am I called Benjamin *Archer*? Shouldn't I be called Benjamin *Manfield*, like him?"

Laura rubbed his shoulders, thinking about her answer. "Well, your Dad was gone so soon. You were just a baby. I knew you wouldn't remember him at all, whereas Grampa took such good care of you... I don't know. I guess it made sense to call you Benjamin Archer." She paused before asking worriedly, "Does that bother you?"

Ben shook his head. "No, not really. I was curious, that's all." She frowned at him, unconvinced. He added quickly, "It's okay, really! I prefer the name Archer; it reminds me of

Grampa."

She hugged him again, so he could not see her biting her lip as she rolled her eyes towards the ceiling. She said gently, "You'd better pack your bags." They glanced at each other. Then she asked, "Are you ready?"

He nodded.

She sighed before opening the door. A wave of human heat and chatter enveloped them as they headed back into the crowd.

* * *

Ben made his way from the kitchen to the stairs, ignoring someone who tapped him on the shoulder. He sprinted up the steps, headed for his bedroom, then froze at the doorway.

A man with short, black hair streaked with grey and wearing a tidy business suit stood near the shelves at the other end of the room, holding a cup of coffee in one hand and Grampa's white telescope in the other. When he realized Ben had arrived, he broke into a toothy grin. "Ah! Here's the boy I was looking for! You must be Benjamin Archer!"

Ben didn't reply.

"She's a beauty, isn't she?" the man

continued, admiring the telescope, while almost splashing coffee on it. "Here, hold this for a minute, would you?" he said, handing the cup to Ben, who had to grab it with both hands as hot liquid dripped onto his arm. Fortunately, the man returned the telescope to its place, still speaking. "Your grandfather and I shared the same passion for the stars. They tell me you do, too." He turned to face Ben. With a smile he put out his hand, presenting himself, "James Hao."

The man's eyes bore into Ben's as he shook it limply, the cup dangerously wavering in his other hand. Hao ignored the cup, saying thoughtfully, "Hm, I'm surprised your grandfather never mentioned me. We go way back, him and me."

Ben scowled. "Were you looking for something?"

Hao's face lit up. "Ah, yes, actually. I spilled coffee on my tie. I was looking for the washroom when I walked by and spotted this beauty." He pointed to the telescope.

"The bathroom is on the other side," Ben said blandly.

Hao straightened. "Indeed!" But instead of leaving, he strolled to the window. "Quite amazing, isn't it, to think meteors crashed into these very fields? I'm sure only a handful of people in the whole world could claim the same. Your grandfather shunned the limelight, yet in a way, he became quite famous in spite of himself. He'll be making the headlines this weekend, too, though obviously for a very unfortunate reason..." Hao walked back over to Ben. "Why, you must have been on vacation when *The Cosmic Fall* occurred! Wouldn't you have loved to be here and witness something like that?" He gazed down at Ben, showing his neat row of teeth.

Ben stared back at him, then returned the cup. Hao carefully took it, holding it at the edges, as if Ben had dirtied it. "Well, you and I must have a chat soon... about the stars," Hao said as he moved towards the door. "See you later, then," he added as he left with a satisfied air.

Yeah, you wish!

Ben shut his bedroom door. He could still hear the man whistling down the corridor.

* * *

On the opposite side, Inspector James Hao locked himself in the bathroom. He stood before the mirror, whistling softly as he emptied the remaining coffee into the sink. He took a plastic bag from an inside pocket, and carefully placed the cup within it. He washed his hands and took his time to plaster down his hair. Still whistling, he tucked the cup in his inside pocket before stepping out. It bulged weirdly, so he glided down the stairs and left the house, walking with large strides to his car. He briefly noted that, although the rain had stopped, it had become very cold. Once inside the vehicle, he placed the cup in the passenger seat before driving away, tires screeching.

CHAPTER 7 *Crystals*

The house emptied slowly. Letting out a sigh of relief, Laura busied herself in the kitchen and noticed the garbage bag was overflowing. She carried it to the kitchen door leading to the backyard. The door squeaked on its old hinges as she pushed it open, cold air taking her by surprise. She went back inside to grab her mother's knitted shawl that always hung on a couch in the living room. She didn't remember it being this cold during the funeral. Although it was early October, it was too early for such a temperature drop.

She left the garbage at the bottom of the four steps outside the kitchen and was heading back inside, when she spotted a tall man in jeans and brown jacket standing with his back to her at the end of the yard, gazing over the fields. She recognized Jack Anderson with his weird fur hat at once.

She wrapped the shawl around her shoulders, took a step forward, then stopped as something crunched under her shoes. She glanced down and found the grass covered in delicate frost crystals. She bent to pick up a fragile, star-shaped crystal that fit in the palm of her hand before joining Jack.

"I hadn't seen one of these in years. It's so beautiful!" she began, before noticing the breathtaking scenery of golden cornfields tumbling down the hillside into the valley below. In the distance, the autumn sun peeked under menacing dark clouds, just above the mountain range. The effect was a mesmerizing, brightly golden sunset in a cold and dark world—a strange sign of summer still clinging in the face of the ever-looming winter.

"My father would have loved this," she said softly.

"I know," Jack replied after a while.

She looked up at him curiously. "You miss him, too, don't you?"

After a short silence, he replied, "Yes."

She studied his handsome features and high

cheekbones. She noticed the small strand of white hair under his fur hat. He stared down at her with deep, honey-brown eyes that reflected pain and exhaustion. "I lost someone, too," he began. "My daughter..." he trailed away as he gazed out at the fields again. "She would have loved this, too."

A dozen raindrops fell on them, accompanied by a handful of very light snowflakes. Laura found herself crying silently, freely and without shame, giving in to her grief almost with relief. She cried for her father and for all the hurtful things they had said to each other. But most of all she cried for the things left unsaid between them. Yet somehow she knew everything was going to be all right, that he forgave her. Just as she forgave him now.

Standing very close to the fur hat man somehow made the cold air more bearable. Her misty breath mingled between the snowflakes and she found herself resisting the urge to take his hand, as natural as it might have seemed in their shared grief, for somehow she knew that if she did so the magic moment between them would evaporate. He had, after all, backed away from her when she had tried to greet him in the graveyard.

Once the sun had sunk behind the mountains, the cornfields became dark, leaving the way for the cold to penetrate through her shawl. Laura gazed into the distance as if hoping to hold back the last ray of sunlight. "I'm glad you came..." she began, turning to Jack, only to find him gone!

She stared in bewilderment at the space where, a moment ago, this mysterious man had been talking to her about his daughter.

"Jack?" she shouted, a chill rippling down her back as the wind picked up and large raindrops spattered on the ground.

But Jack Anderson had gone.

* * *

It didn't take Inspector James Hao long to get to the rendezvous point at a crossroad that led to Chilliwack. He found the white, unmarked van parked under some trees by the side of a lonely road.

Hao knocked on the van door to be let in by one of his men. He placed the cup in the agent's hands, ordering, "Get the fingerprints on this cup analyzed pronto and have them compared to the ones we found on the broken glass we recovered from the crash site."

The agent nodded.

Connelly and a second agent were in deep discussion, poring over the computer screens, only pausing when Hao came up behind them.

"What is it?" Hao asked.

The second agent looked up at him. "We may be onto something. Watch this."

He pulled up a photograph of the funeral from that morning. It depicted a general picture of the graveyard, with autumn trees and lush grass, while in the distance a group of mourners gathered around Ryan Archer's grave. Some people strolled away, while others lined up to pay their respects to Laura Archer. At this distance, people's faces appeared small and blurry. Zooming in was the only way to get a better idea of people's identities.

"Agent Connelly noticed this in the corner," the agent explained as he zoomed into the left side of the picture, away from the crowd, slowly bringing Hao's attention to a dog standing by a tree. The agent zoomed out again so that a boy appeared next to the dog.

"That's Archer's grandson," Hao stated.

The agent nodded. "Yes, but look at this."

He moved the angle of the picture slightly so that Hao could make out the face of a man with a fur hat between the branches of surrounding shrubs. The boy seemed to be conversing with him.

"Who's that?" Hao asked swiftly.

Connelly spoke. "We've identified most of the people who attended the funeral. They are regular Chilliwack folk. But not this guy, though."

Hao snapped, "Are you telling me we don't have him in the system?"

"We're still searching."

"I want to know who that is! Find me a name!" Hao ordered. "We'll go back to the motel and work on this all night if we have to!" He pointed to Connelly. "And you! You're keeping watch. Report to me immediately if the Archer woman or her son leave the house!"

* * *

Connelly settled in the Nissan as the other men took off in the van. He sat back, crossed his arms and kept his eyes on the road before him. The rain thinned, making it easier for him to make out the people who passed in their cars. On a typical day there would have been very little traffic coming to and from the country road where Ryan Archer's house stood, as there were few neighbours, but on this late afternoon, the last of the reception visitors headed back to Chilliwack. Connelly watched as a man, covered in a large plastic bag and wearing a beanie hat, cycled by, glancing at him briefly. Connelly glared at him, unmoving, until he was far gone. Because of this, he almost missed the red Dodge Grand Caravan that slowed as it reached the stop sign of the crossroad.

Connelly could barely make out the woman driver and, next to her, a boy. A small dog's face stared out at him from the rear window. Connelly straightened, fully alert. It was the same dog as in the graveyard picture. He switched on the engine and followed the Dodge as it turned onto the highway heading to Vancouver, without informing his superior.

* * *

Laura Archer woke up to a grey morning, feeling refreshed and rested. She realized she hadn't had a regular night's sleep in a long time and the funeral had left her completely drained.

She showered, then put on some black slacks, a white top, a large, grey sweater with a V-neck, black ballerina flats and a pendant she had inherited from her mother. She brushed her shoulder-length hair, pinning it back into a ponytail, then headed downstairs, half expecting to hear her father's loud roar of laughter as she entered the kitchen. She swallowed hard when only silence greeted her. Still, it felt good to be in her childhood home with its full windows and wooden beams in the white ceiling. While she brewed some coffee, she wandered around the living room, stroking the furniture with the tips of her fingers, gazing at old photographs. She was struck by how quiet it was. Once upon a time, she would have rejected the lack of sound, she would have yearned for the bustling of the city, yet now found the calm strangely relaxing.

She headed back to the kitchen to pour herself a cup of the black brew. While sipping on the hot liquid, she leaned against the wall, then stared out the window towards the empty yard, catching herself thinking of Jack Anderson again and wondering how he could have disappeared so suddenly. Shaking her head to get him out of her mind, Laura washed the cup before leaving it to dry, then checked her handbag to make sure she had her wallet, identity cards, keys, some makeup and, most importantly, her asthma inhaler. After putting on her coat and a light shawl, she locked the door, then headed out into the chilly morning.

By 9:25 a.m., Laura had parked on Knight Road in downtown Chilliwack. She crossed the road, only to realize the notary's office was further up than she expected. She picked up the pace when a homeless man with his face hiding behind a thick scarf made her slow down. He jingled coins in a plastic cup at her. Automatically, she reached into her purse, and dropped some coins into the cup as she walked by—as her father had taught her to do since childhood.

As the homeless man with the beany hat saluted her with his hand covered in fingerless gloves, she heard him say, "You're like your daddy, you are."

She turned in surprise, then stopped as she recognized Wayne the Bagman—the homeless man who had spoken to her the day before at the funeral reception. "Hi," she said awkwardly, walking away more slowly.

He looked at her intently. "Where's that boy of yours? You shouldn't leave him alone, you know?"

"What do you mean?"

"It's not safe," he said as she distanced herself from him. "You need to take him away. Far away!"

Laura glared at him, then decided to ignore

him. She had reached the notary's office and pushed the commercial glass doors inward.

"I wouldn't go in there if I were you!" Wayne shouted after her.

Laura frowned at him angrily, stepping inside.

She chose the stairs over the elevator to go up to the first floor, where she entered the reception office that had a sign on the front: CHARLES BOYLE, NOTARY PUBLIC. A couple sat in the waiting area, reading magazines.

A thirty-something-year-old assistant with short, brown hair stopped typing on her computer and smiled at her.

"Good morning," Laura said, smiling back. "I have an appointment with Mr. Boyle at 9:30. My name is Laura Archer."

The woman's smile evaporated, her face turning to panic. She stuttered, "Oh... but you're not supposed to be here..."

Laura stared at her in bewilderment. "Excuse me?" She recognized the woman's voice. "You called me a couple of days ago, after my father passed away, asking me to come in today!"

The assistant, who had been calmly working a minute ago, now seemed totally at a loss as to what to do. "I... er... you must have misunderstood.

The notary is not in today," she stammered.

Laura stood with her mouth open in disbelief. She pointed to the couple sitting in the waiting room. "What about them? Who are they waiting for?" The couple stared back at them curiously.

The assistant's eyes widened as she searched for an answer, but then muffled laughter came from the notary's office.

"Who's in there?" Laura asked angrily.

As the assistant opened her mouth to reply, Laura strode to the office door while the woman struggled to get out of her chair. "Wait!" she warned, but already Laura had opened the door to peek inside.

Two men, one of them with neat, graying hair, the other with thick glasses and a big belly, stood beside the notary's desk, laughing at a joke.

"We must plan another round of golf..." the man with the graying hair said, before stopping to find out who had interrupted the meeting. For a brief moment his eyes narrowed, before creasing into a smile. "Ms. Archer, what a pleasant surprise!" he said nimbly, nodding towards the assistant who stood behind Laura. He reached out his hand. "I'm Charles Boyle," he presented himself.

Laura shook the man's hand unhappily.

Boyle gestured to the chair before his desk, inviting her to sit. Then he turned to the plump man, leading him politely but firmly out the door. "I'm sorry, Mr. Smith, my assistant is reminding me of an urgent meeting I must attend. She will go over my agenda with you so we can finalize the paperwork as soon as possible. It was a pleasure catching up with you, as always."

They shook hands, then, as the client turned away, Laura saw the notary giving his assistant instructions which implied making a phone call, to which she hastily nodded in understanding. He closed the door, calmly returned to his desk, sat and crossed the fingers of his hands on the table in front of him in a business-like manner. "Ms. Archer," he said gravely. "We don't have much time."

"What's going on here?" Laura said in bewilderment.

Boyle inspected her curiously. "You did not bring your son along?" he asked.

Laura shook her head. "No, I sent him home. His grandfather's passing has not been easy on him."

Boyle nodded in approval. "Good," he said slowly, lost in thought. "Still, out of respect for your late father—may he rest in peace—I must warn you that my assistant is calling the police."

"What?" Laura exclaimed, perplexed. "Why?"

"Have you heard of the CSIS, Ms. Archer?" Boyle asked.

Laura blinked at him, racking her brain. "You mean, the Canadian version of the FBI?"

"Yes," Boyle acknowledged. "Well, you see, a couple of their agents barged into my office yesterday, waving a lot of official documents at my face." He gazed at her intently. "I intended to read your father's will to you this morning, as he had instructed me to do at his passing, but yesterday's unexpected visitors changed everything. You see, your father's assets have been frozen. The CSIS has taken hold of your father's will as well as his inheritance."

"What?" Laura burst, incredulous. "But why? Is that even legal?"

"Last week I would have said 'no.' I have never experienced anything similar," he said. "But, as it turns out, I was wrong. They did this in all legality. I'm afraid, Ms. Archer, that I am unable to read your father's will to you today."

Laura stared at him, her mind unable to grasp what he was saying.

Boyle continued apologetically, "To be

honest, my assistant and I did not expect you in today. We... er... I guess we expected the CSIS to have made you aware of the situation by now. It was our error... we should have contacted you immediately." He pulled open a side drawer and dug out a medium-sized envelope. "Nevertheless," he continued. "I am glad you came, as they did not get their hands on this." He handed the brown envelope to Laura, who took it with a look of total confusion. He said gently, "Don't think I approve of what is happening, Ms. Archer. Your father's passing is a loss to us all. The community greatly appreciated him, myself included." His voice lowered to a hush. "This envelope was not part of the will. Your father entrusted it to me, as one friend to another, and made me promise to give it to you should you ever face any trouble. Please, do not mention this envelope to anyone. It is the only thing of your father's that I was able to... how shall I say... omit from yesterday's investigation."

Laura sat like a statue, gaping at the envelope dazedly.

The notary stood, saying gravely, "However, I can't ignore the arrest warrant that came in this morning. That is why it is my duty to call the police, Ms. Archer. So I beg you: leave quickly!"

Laura's handbag tumbled to the ground as

she shoved back her chair. "An arrest warrant? Why?" she asked, fumbling to pick up the handbag. "I've done nothing wrong!"

Boyle stared at her in surprise. "No, not for you!" he said. "It's for your son. The arrest warrant is for your son!"

Laura gaped at him in horror.

CHAPTER 8 *The First Witness*

At dawn that morning, Inspector Hao had received new information from the Dugout about the fur hat man in the funeral photograph. Surveillance cameras at the Toronto airport showed him arriving a week ago from South America, travelling with a Canadian passport that identified him as Jack Anderson. However, as it turned out, the Bolivian Embassy had informed Canadian authorities two days ago that the real Jack Anderson had fallen to his death attempting to walk the dangerous Inca Trail. His remains were being flown back to Canada that same day. Meaning that the CSIS had no clue as to the real identity of the fur hat man, nor how he had managed to travel across the country from

Toronto to Chilliwack without leaving a trace.

On the other hand, the fingerprints that Hao had gotten from Benjamin Archer at the funeral reception matched those on the pieces of glass recovered from the crash site, officially turning the boy into a previously unknown witness of *The Cosmic Fall*. Not to mention that Ben was the last person to have spoken to the fur hat man. It was high time they interrogated Benjamin Archer.

Hao had rushed to Ryan Archer's house, only to find it empty. Quite conveniently, though, they had received a call from the local RCMP informing them that Laura Archer was currently at the notary on Knight Road.

"Has Connelly reported back yet?" Hao fumed, as one of the agents parked the white van.

"Not yet," the other agent replied, checking his phone for messages.

Hao swore as they searched the other side of the road with their eyes.

"There she is!" the agent who was driving the van said. They watched as Laura Archer left the notary's building.

"The boy's not with her!" Hao exclaimed.

The three men got out of the van. They swiftly crossed the road, closing in on Ben's mother.

* * *

Laura saw them at once, running towards her in their dark grey suits. One of them flashed a badge at her. "Laura Archer? I'm Inspector James Hao with the CSIS. We need to talk to you."

She glanced around desperately.

"In here!" someone shouted urgently. Startled, Laura turned around to find a man peeking out at her from a narrow back alley. It was Wayne the Bagman urging her to come to him. Following a wild, baffling hunch, Laura ran to the homeless man.

"Hold it!" Hao yelled. But already she had slipped into the back alley after Wayne who was holding a metal door open for her. She dove into darkness and heard the door shut behind her.

"This way!" Wayne urged. Laura realized they were in a dimly lit corridor. The sound of thumping fists hastened her on.

The homeless man turned out to be much fitter than he seemed, for with a swift stride he led her up several flights of stairs to a closed emergency exit. Wayne pushed it open, and Laura found herself on a small, rusty bridge structure between two brick buildings above another back alley. A key materialized in Wayne's hand from under his rags and in no time the door to the next building opened. He ushered her through it so that, again, they were faced with corridors and stairways. Laura's head swam as she lost all sense of direction, while they ran up and down flights of stairs until Wayne led her to a garage with a yellowish Buick stationed there. He ran to the garage door to pull it open, then unlocked the car door on the driver's side before taking his place behind the wheel. "Get in!" he ordered.

Laura froze to the spot, fear gripping her heart. "Wait!" she urged. "I can't do this! What am I doing? This is insane! I'm running away from the police. I've done nothing wrong."

"It's not you they're after!" Wayne said impatiently. "They're after your son. You have to get to him before they do." Since she continued to hesitate, he barked, "Get into the car!"

Automatically, she obeyed, her breath coming in short gasps. He put the key in the ignition, the car spurted to life, and before long Laura found herself heading out of town, racing down the highway.

Once they were satisfied that no one was following them, she turned to Wayne. "What do they want Ben for?"

He glanced at her, saying nothing.

"And what about you? What have you got to do with any of this? Why are you helping me?" she insisted.

The man did not reply, concentrating on his driving.

"I'm talking to you!" Laura yelled. She was on the verge of a full-blown asthma attack.

Wayne did not seem affected by her outburst. "I always knew your father had made a mistake by not involving you. He was hoping to protect you from all this, but they were bound to find out about you sooner or later." He shook his head disapprovingly. "He should have known better."

Laura stared at him angrily, not appreciating his comments. She grabbed the wheel, veering it sharply to the right. He hit the brakes so hard the tires screeched.

"What's the matter with you?" he yelled through his thick, unkempt beard.

"I'm not letting go until you tell me what's going on!" she seethed, still grasping the wheel. Cars honked as they sped past on the highway.

"Yeah, all right!" he growled. "Now let go!"

Laura did as he asked, and he carefully wove his way back into the fast lane, muttering furiously under his breath.

"What's your name?" she demanded firmly.

"Wayne McGuillen. Professional homeless man, at your service!"

Laura glared at him. He didn't appear to be joking.

"Why are these people after my son?"

Wayne looked at her curiously again. "You don't know, do you?" She frowned at him to get on with it. "It's because of *The Cosmic Fall*, of course."

"The Cosmic Fall?" she said, incredulous. "What does that have to do with anything?"

He replied slowly, "Well, your son was there, on the night of *The Fall*. He witnessed everything."

Laura felt goosebumps on her skin. She remained silent, trying not to show that she was embarrassed not to know more about her son's involvement on that fateful night. She said, "Yes, I'm aware my son witnessed the fall of some pretty big meteors next to my father's property. I understand that this was a terrifying ordeal for him, but that doesn't explain why the police are after him."

Wayne stared at her before saying slowly, "The thing is, it wasn't meteors that fell into the woods that night. It was alien spacecraft."

Laura felt her breath shortening again. She closed her eyes to fend off the asthma crisis threatening to take over. She did not want to show any signs of weakness by reaching for her inhaler, so she forced herself to take long, deep breaths to calm down. "You're making that up. Everybody knows those were meteors. The news showed how they recovered the meteor debris from the fields. Why would you make up such a story?"

He answered slowly, "Because I was there, too. I saw them: the UFOs and the aliens. I saw all of it. As did your father, your son, and two others. There were five witnesses in all..." he trailed off, remembering. "Five civil witnesses, yet only four of us were picked up by the CSIS. Somehow they missed your son. Your father managed to hide him from them. A good thing, too! They brought us in for questioning. We thought they only needed us to file a witness report. Instead, they kept us locked away for weeks! They used the excuse that we might have been exposed to alien viruses and were dangerous to the public. In fact, they were afraid we would talk to the press. They went to great lengths to cover up the truth, which is why we were considered a menace." Laura could hear the hurt in his voice. "All I wanted was to be left alone for a quiet night's sleep in the woods. Instead, I found myself locked up for weeks, prodded like a guinea pig as if I were the alien."

Laura listened to him without moving, unsure what to make of his words. She couldn't tell if this man in ragged clothes had completely lost it, which was all the more alarming as he sounded so sincere. "Yet, here you are, safe and sound…" she said carefully.

Wayne didn't seem to mind her statement. "Somehow your father got word to the Canadian Human Rights Commission, and they were forced to release us in great secrecy, with tons of signed papers saying we would not reveal anything to any living soul. That's what they did officially, though behind closed doors, they bugged our houses and followed us day in and day out. That's when your father stepped in again. He helped us disappear from the police radar by finding us places to hide. He provided us with a new life so they would leave us alone.

"I went into the Yukon for a while. Couldn't take the cold. Came back to my hometown where I continued living rough. Kept an eye on your Dad. I knew he came into town incognito once in a while to sort things out for his family and the other witnesses."

He glanced at Laura again before adding, "Good thing I did, too. Found him by his car when he had his heart attack. Dropped him off at the hospital along with your phone number. But I guess I was too late..."

Laura stared at him sadly. His story made sense, yet at the same time sounded completely crazy. Part of her was very reluctant to accept anything he said because admitting it meant a huge weight falling on her shoulders. It was much easier to brush him off as mad. And yet he had helped her dad...

Suddenly, Wayne veered off the highway into a small dirt road leading through fields. Not long after, he turned into a lot filled with shrubs and a low, run-down house where white paint still showed through the cracked and peeling walls. In a swift movement, he pulled into a dusty garage before turning off the engine.

"What are you doing?" Laura asked, her suspicion growing tenfold.

"This is my stop," Wayne said.

Laura stared at him in bewilderment.

He threw the car key into her lap before getting out.

"Wait! What...?"

"This is as far as I go," he interrupted. "I did my part, paid my debt to your father. Go and get your son, Laura. Take the car. It was your father's anyway."

Laura slid into the driver's seat, then mechanically tried to get the key into the ignition. Her hands shook. "Wait a minute! Is that it? What am I supposed to do now? Where am I supposed to go?" She had so many questions, but at the same time, she wanted to get away as fast as possible.

"Don't trust anyone," he said, echoing her very thoughts.

She barely had time to back nervously out of the garage when he started pulling down the garage door.

"Hide! Like me," she heard him say, as the door shut firmly, obscuring her view of him. And just like that, he was gone.

Laura stared at the silent house. She was in a cold sweat, her foot trembling on the pedal. She remembered the Inspector's face as he lunged at her. He was real. The arrest warrant for her son was real. Ben's face flickered before her eyes and she strengthened her grip on the wheel. He was all she had, all that mattered. She did not want those CSIS men to come anywhere near her son. Feeling a wave of urgency wash over her, she pushed down on the pedal, and sped off, leaving the lonely man to his wild imagination.

* * *

After an unproductive search for Laura Archer and her mysterious saviour, Inspector James Hao entered the notary's office with his notebook in hand. As he drilled Charles Boyle about Laura and her son's whereabouts, he spotted something jutting out from under the notary's desk. It turned out to be an asthma inhaler with Laura Archer's name on it. He knew it required a doctor's prescription. Hao gazed out the window thoughtfully before putting the asthma inhaler safely in his pocket.

CHAPTER 9 *The Trap*

Almost sixty miles away, Ben stared out his classroom window, daydreaming. Concentrating on the lessons proved an impossible task.

He had made it to school on time that morning, thanks to the very obliging Mrs. Ghallagher from Chilliwack. Not only had she driven him back to Vancouver, she had also insisted he spend the night at her daughter's house, as she would not hear of him staying on his own after losing his grandfather so recently. He had found himself in an elegant family home on a tree-lined avenue in a well-to-do neighbourhood, with Mrs. Ghallagher's daughter, husband and three-year-old daughter. He had reluctantly joined their joyful, bustling family dinner before settling in a cozy guest room all to himself. However, they would not hear of Tike sleeping in the bedroom with him. This thorny issue had almost turned into a nasty conversation until Ben had unwillingly relented. Then, as soon as everyone was sleeping soundly, the boy had silently opened the kitchen door for his happy four-legged friend. They had huddled up close before falling fast asleep.

The next morning, Tike had scuttled under the bed before Mrs. Ghallagher came to wake Ben up. After a hasty breakfast, she had ushered him into the car again so she could take him to school.

While Mrs. Ghallager was distracted by her granddaughter crying in the back seat, Ben was able to convince her that his mom was picking him up that afternoon; therefore, he did not need to spend another night at the daughter's house. She dropped him off at the main school entrance with his dog, backpack and a small suitcase, and watched until he entered the school building. Only then had he been able to breathe.

Fortunately, most teachers left him alone that day, though Ben's science teacher offered his condolences. Still, it turned out to be one of the slowest school days he could remember, worsening when he was in a classroom that allowed him to catch a glimpse of Tike waiting patiently outside in the rain. More than anything else, Ben longed to be with his dog, who offered him his only solace.

On one occasion he found himself staring outside again while his companions listened resolutely to the teacher when he noticed Tike standing still as stone, ears alert, one paw off the ground, like a hunting dog sensing its prey. Then slowly his tail lowered between his legs, indicating fear as if the prey had turned out to be a predator. Ben sat up, feeling alert for the first time that day. He followed the direction of Tike's gaze, immediately spotting what had caught the dog's attention.

A bald man was posted by the gates at the end of the playground, observing the school. Ben could not make out his features from this far, yet he broke into a cold sweat. He glanced around the classroom to see if anyone else sensed danger, but the other students worked placidly on their assignments. By the time he looked back, Tike was sitting again, though straight and alert, and the man was gone.

If he had not been able to concentrate before, it now became near to impossible. Earlier he had been in a sad, dreamy state, now he was alert and nervous, checking on Tike every two minutes. Ben was so focused on what was happening outside that he jumped when someone knocked on the classroom door. An assistant from the school reception came in. She whispered something to the teacher before turning to find Ben.

"Benjamin?" she said. "Could you come with me, please? And, bring your backpack with you."

Ben stood so fast his chair almost fell over. He crammed his books into his backpack, asking, as he followed her out, "What's going on?"

"There's a phone call for you. You can take it in the Principal's office," the woman said as she led him to the reception area.

The Principal's assistant glanced up as she spoke over the phone. "Yes, Ms. Archer, he's here. Please accept my condolences for the loss of your father." She nodded into the receiver before adding, "Yes, goodbye." She handed the receiver to Ben, saying, "It's your mother."

Ben took it from her, relieved. "Mom?"

His mother answered hurriedly on the other end. "I'm here to pick you up. Can you come right away? I'm on the side street to the right of the school."

"Ok. Hold on," he replied, eyeing the stern

assistant. "My mom is here to pick me up. Is it okay if..." he began.

The assistant said, "Yes, yes, she told me."

"I'll be right there, Mom," Ben said into the receiver before hanging up. "Thank you," he said to the assistant, who ushered him out with a wave of her hand. "Make sure to let us know when you'll be back at school, Benjamin."

Ben nodded, already halfway out the door. He ran outside with his backpack thumping at his side. He whistled to Tike who joined him with his tongue lolling and tail wagging. Suddenly, Ben stopped in his tracks.

My suitcase!

He had forgotten his suitcase with his clothes and toothbrush upstairs. He wondered briefly whether he should go back for it, but rapidly decided against it. He wanted to see his Mom.

I wonder why she's in such a hurry to pick me up?

He sped along the school wall, then out the side gate into the short street he had taken not so long ago to escape the two bullies. He walked at a fast pace, searching for his mother's car, then jumped when he passed a chain link fence. He had completely forgotten about the three guard dogs who prowled up and down the yard as if they had been waiting for him all afternoon. He tried not to pay attention to them but couldn't avoid feeling their dark eyes fixated on his every step. So much so, that he did not notice the bald man heading across the street straight towards him. It was only because Tike bounced back into him with his tail between his legs that he suddenly realized what was happening.

The man was almost on top of him, reaching out to grab him.

"Wha...?" Ben exclaimed, stepping back in fright. He didn't have time to finish his sentence, as he lost his balance and fell backwards into the sloping parking entrance next to the guard dogs' house.

The three beasts barked ferociously, throwing themselves at the fence.

Ben's breath was knocked out of him as he hit the ground. Fortunately, his backpack broke most of the impact, though he scraped his elbows.

Already the man reached out for him again. Tike tugged at the assailant's pants, but the man kicked him aside nonchalantly.

Ben blinked the stars from his eyes and rolled over swiftly. He dropped his backpack and slid further down into the dark, public parking structure. He ran down to the second and last level, splashing through the large rain puddle that had trickled down the ramp and accumulated at the bottom. Only a couple of cars were parked there with no one in sight who could help. Ben ran to the end of the parking lot, knowing full well it was useless, for there was no other way out.

Behind him the man followed more slowly, knowing he had Ben cornered. The guard dogs' hysterical barking echoed into the parking lot.

Tike hid behind Ben's legs. Ben had his back against the concrete wall, facing the man in the grey suit. It was the same man he had spotted from his classroom window that afternoon.

"Leave me alone!" Ben shouted at him.

The man continued to approach until he was a couple of strides away. He gazed, bemused, at the terrier who bared his teeth in an attempt to protect Ben, though not a bark or growl left his throat.

Ben thought it was a trick of the light, but he was sure he had just seen the man's eyes switch colour. He caught his breath.

Twisted eyes!

Then, to Ben's horror, the being's whole face began to tremble at an alarming speed, as if two identities struggled to take control of his features. When the unnatural shaking stopped, instead of the bald man with green eyes who had been there before, there now stood a taller man with spiky, white hair and honey-brown eyes. The being clenched his teeth, as if he were angry with his own transformation.

Ben yelled urgently, "Mom! Mom!"

The being turned his face away, a smile on the corner of his mouth, and Ben heard his mother say, "I'm right here, honey!" Then the being looked at Ben again as his mother's voice left his lips, "I told you I'd pick you up."

Ben's heart dropped like a stone, his skin crawling as if a hundred tiny spiders were skittering up and down his body. He stared at the abnormal man with dread. The being had spoken with Laura Archer's voice, the same one that he had heard in the receiver in the school office.

"Where... where's my mother? What did you do to her?" Ben's voice came out thick with fear.

The being didn't seem amused anymore. "I'm not here to talk about your mother, Benjamin Archer."

How does he know my name?

He stared intently at the boy, then said, "I'm here to talk about Mesmo."

Ben caught his breath. "I don't know what you're talking about," he croaked, his voice sounding weak and unconvincing.

The being was unsmiling. "Of course you do. You see, your grandfather and I talked about you four days ago."

Ben's eyes widened, his mind whirling back as something clicked in his memory. He had bumped into this man in the hospital after visiting Grampa that night, though back then he had been wearing a doctor's coat.

The night Grampa passed away...

Ben stared at the unnatural man with new fear in his eyes. "Who are you?" he breathed. Somewhere far away, the guard dogs barked incessantly.

"I am Bordock, also known as the Shapeshifter. That is my skill," the being said enigmatically. "I have been playing a hide-and-seek game with Mesmo for almost two months, and my patience is running out." His dark eyes bored into Ben's. "You spoke to Mesmo yesterday, in the graveyard, during the funeral. Why?"

Ben swallowed hard.

How can he know that?

Why did he feel smaller and smaller while Bordock loomed ever larger over him? Ben unconsciously reached for Grampa's watch, silently praying it would magically make him disappear.

"I don't understand what you want," Ben said helplessly. "Leave me alone!"

The Shapeshifter grabbed him by the shirt, glaring down at him. His eyes were deep, brown pools that stirred another memory in Ben's mind, one that was terrifying: something that had triggered many nightmares and which he had tucked far away into his unconscious.

"I want Mesmo," the Shapeshifter said menacingly. "And you're going to tell me where he is!"

"I'm right here, Bordock," a voice boomed from behind them.

Ben peeked from behind the Shapeshifter's shoulder as he turned around slowly.

Mesmo stood at the bottom of the ramp, his tall body reflected in the large puddle of rain.

The Shapeshifter let go of Ben's shirt, then placed himself before him, so that Ben had to stretch his neck to see what was going on.

The two men glared at each other with palpable hate.

"Finally!" Bordock said. "What took you so long?"

"Leave the boy alone, Bordock," Mesmo said. "He has nothing to do with this."

Bordock observed Ben curiously for a second, before jeering, "What would you care about an Earthling boy, Mesmo? Have you lost track of your mission?"

"That's enough! You've done enough harm already!" Mesmo retorted.

"Not quite enough," Bordock said darkly, before adding slowly, "You're still here." He braced himself as the air filled with static, which drew to him like a magnet. An invisible force gathered around the Shapeshifter. His hands and arms began to glow.

In that instant, a car screeched into the parking entrance before coming to an abrupt stop. The car door opened and a woman stepped out. She bent to pick up Ben's backpack.

"Ben?" Laura called.

"Mom!" Ben cried back frantically.

The Shapeshifter launched a powerful ball of blue light straight at Mesmo who dropped down, placed his hands in the giant puddle then turned it into a solid, transparent shield that blew into a thousand fragments as it was hit straight on. The air fizzled and cracked, transforming into a fine mixture of mist and smoke.

Mesmo picked himself up.

Bordock grinned as he gathered energy; blue

light emanating from his hands and arms again. But he froze suddenly when vicious barking boomed into the parking lot. The three massive dogs from next door dashed down the ramp and emerged out of the mist. They headed straight for Bordock and the boy. In seconds they would be upon Ben. His mother cried out in alarm. Ben put up his arms to protect his face, shouting, "Stop!"

Incredibly, they did.

The three beasts froze in their tracks right in front of Bordock, growling at him menacingly, searching for the slightest movement. They circled him, shaking with anticipation, barely containing their urge to pounce.

Ben remained stuck to the concrete wall, afraid to move an inch for fear they would turn their attention to him.

The mist dissipated, while everyone waited cautiously, mesmerized by the deep growling creatures circling the being in the grey suit.

When nothing happened, Bordock let out a hissing breath. He frowned angrily, saying through gritted teeth, "What is this? How is this possible?"

Mesmo, joined by Laura, seemed equally perplexed.

"This is not your doing! It cannot be!"

Bordock snarled. "And your daughter's skill died with her! Unless..." he stiffened abruptly. Then, as if a silent message had passed between them, both Bordock and Mesmo turned their attention to Ben at the same time, a look of utter disbelief in their eyes.

Ben swallowed, shaking his head in confusion.

Bordock's eyes narrowed as if he were seeing Ben for the first time; the boy could see his mind was trying to comprehend the incomprehensible.

"Ben!" his mother called anxiously.

Her voice came through to him. Carefully, Ben extracted himself from between the wall and the man. He distanced himself from the Shapeshifter slowly, afraid he would lunge. But all he did was glare fiercely.

The air was static, the few dim lights flickered, as Mesmo urged, "Hurry!"

Laura grabbed Ben's shoulders in a kind of urgent hug, then pushed him ahead of her. The three sprinted up the ramp. Ben opened the back door of the car, jumped in, and was closely followed by Mesmo and Tike. Laura pushed their door shut as she got in. In an instant, the motor came to life. The car screeched backwards into the street, leaving Bordock to his fate.

CHAPTER 10 *Lighthouse Park*

They drove through the city, making it out before the start of rush hour, then crossed Lion's Gate Bridge to the north shore, which joined the Sea-to-Sky Highway going west. Laura checked her rear-view mirror constantly to make sure nobody was following them. Instead, she caught Jack Anderson staring intently at Ben.

When Ben put a hand to his forehead, saying, "Mom, I feel dizzy!" she veered sharply into a driveway leading to the forested coast, which soon turned into a dirt road surrounded by old, majestic red cedars with a sign that read Lighthouse Park. She stopped the car in the visitor parking lot in the middle of a lush forest, which was almost empty of tourists at this time of the season, then got out of the car hurriedly.

"What are you doing, Mom?" Ben asked.

She opened the back door, ordering, "You! Get out!" She pointed to Jack. He obeyed. She then closed and locked the doors by clicking on her car keys to keep Ben safe inside.

"Mom!" he objected, knocking on the window.

She took no notice of him as she faced Jack. "You!" she repeated. "Jack... or whatever your name is... You'd better tell me what's going on or I'm leaving without you this instant!"

Ben thumped on the car window.

"Stay right there, Ben, until I've sorted this out!" she ordered. She glared at Jack, both angry and afraid at the same time. "I've been chased around all morning by the police and now... this! Whatever this was!" She waved her hand in the general direction of the city, shaking her head, then continued without waiting for an answer. "Wayne was right. I'm taking Ben far away from here!"

"Bordock will look for you," Jack warned. "He will never stop. Not after what just happened."

Laura grimaced, "Don't you dare make this about us! We don't have anything to do with this Bordock—nor with you for that matter. Both of you leave us alone!" She reached for the car door.

Jack bent to the ground.

"What are you doing?" she asked fearfully.

He touched a small puddle with his index finger. The water crackled and turned into a beautiful ice crystal with intricate designs, like the ones she had seen at her father's house after his funeral.

She stared at the crystal, taken back to that beautiful, golden sunset over the fields, the grass crunching with fresh, delicate ice... She felt a calm wash over her instantly.

After a silence, she breathed, "Who are you?"

Ben banged on the door again. "Mom," his voice sounded muffled. Still staring at the ice crystal, Laura opened the door for him as if in a trance. Ben stepped out before she could change her mind. "Before Grampa died, he told me to find Mesmo if we were ever in trouble." He pointed up at the tall man, and added, "This is Mesmo."

Laura and Ben both stared at the stranger with his out-of-place fur hat until Laura ventured, "Then who is Jack Anderson?"

Mesmo shook his head sadly. "The real Jack Anderson died in a mountain climbing accident in Bolivia last week. I borrowed his name." He turned his attention to Ben. "Something happened in the parking lot—something I can't quite explain." He paused before continuing, "I'm going to need you to recover your memory about the night of *The Cosmic Fall.*"

Ben gasped. "But you said you didn't want me to."

"Today changed everything. Your grandfather wanted you to forget—to protect you—but after what happened today, that is no longer possible. Bordock was after me. Now he is going to go after you, too."

"Hold on a minute!" Laura interjected. "What would you know about *The Cosmic Fall?*"

Mesmo held her gaze before answering, "I was the one who crashed that night."

Laura pointed a stern finger at him. "Hold it right there, Mister! Don't come to me with some crazy story about crashed UFO's. I heard that one already..." She caught her breath as her eyes fell on the ice crystal.

Mesmo explained. "Bordock shot down our spacecraft. My daughter and two of my companions perished. Somehow I survived. Your father found me and saved me by carrying me to his house. But the police picked him up after he went back to help my companions. I took Ben and escaped."

Laura gasped, something clicking in her mind. "Are you saying you carried Ben from my father's house all the way to Chilliwack that night?"

"Yes," Mesmo replied.

Laura stared at him with a mixture of awe and fear.

Ben grabbed his mother's arm and pleaded, "Mom, I need to remember!"

Laura shook her head. "I don't know if that's a good idea, Ben. Besides, I wouldn't know how to do that. You know we've tried."

Ben turned to Mesmo. "Can you help me?"

"Yes."

* * *

The three of them sat on a small beach surrounded by boulders topped with fir trees. Way above, the white and red lighthouse illuminated the bay, while in the distance the lights of Vancouver glittered under the night sky.

Laura had had the presence of mind to check the trunk of her father's car, which contained two ragged blankets, some camping gear, a first aid kit, some cans of food, and instant coffee. Amazed at her father's foresight, she thanked him silently for having taught her how to start a fire when she was a girl. She warmed up a can of beans, which she and Ben devoured, though Mesmo would not touch it. They had found a plastic bottle in a garbage bin, then filled it with water from a tap placed at the park entrance for tourists visiting the site. The water was beginning to boil in the bean can. She would mix some instant coffee in it.

The stars became brighter, while a soft wind blew as they stared at the embers, thinking of the events of the day.

Mesmo interrupted their thoughts. "It is time."

Ben and Laura glanced at him expectantly.

Then, before they could do anything, Mesmo plunged his whole hand into the boiling water. "No!" Laura yelled in horror. Ben stood up in haste.

Mesmo did not flinch. Before their very eyes, the water bulged out of the can until it formed a perfectly flat, elliptical shape, quite like a mirror, except that you could see through it. Ben and Laura stared with their mouths open.

"How did you do that?" Laura asked in awe.

"My skill is *water*," Mesmo said, as if that

explained everything. "Come," he said to Ben, motioning for him to sit behind the floating mirror. "Touch the water with the tips of your fingers," Mesmo instructed. "It will not hurt."

Ben did as he was told, half expecting to be burnt, but all he felt was the cool liquid under his fingertips.

"Close your eyes and go back as far as you can to the night of *The Cosmic Fall*," Mesmo said. "Try to picture it in your mind."

Ben shifted uneasily, trying to remember something from before, but as usual everything from that time was a dark haze in his mind. Tike, with his tail wagging slowly, placed his paw on Ben's leg. Immediately an image of a baby dog yapping excitedly appeared behind Ben's eyelids. He heard his mother gasp. He snapped his eyes open to find the same image of a barking Tike emerging like a reflection on the water mirror, as though it was a strange TV screen reflecting his thoughts. The image wavered. Mesmo urged him to keep concentrating.

Ben focused on baby Tike, remembering when Grampa had let him into his room one summer when he was six years old. It was a beautiful memory, one that made him smile, but then the image wavered as his grandfather's face lingered in his mind. He opened his eyes again, noticing that his mother's lips were pressed together. He shifted uneasily. Mesmo encouraged him to continue. But Ben could not get past that one memory, as it played over and over in his mind. He looked at Mesmo helplessly.

Mesmo reached out to the transparent screen, touching it with the tip of his finger. It came to life at once.

The alien man sat in an unusual vehicle with soft lights and smooth walls. Outside, everything was dark until the craft glided to the right. The Earth appeared, vast and majestic. He was following another identical craft with which he exchanged strange words. The soft, disciplined voice that came back belonged to a girl. They gently navigated their spacecraft ever closer to the Blue Planet. Then a sharp flash of light zoomed from behind them, almost hitting the first vessel.

The girl's voice burst in warning. Mesmo exchanged urgent words with her as he steered the craft around to see from where the shot had come. No sooner had he done that, when two more shots were fired from a dark spacecraft behind them. One shot flew past, crashing into the American communication satellite, which exploded. The other hit Mesmo's ship with full force, making it shudder as it spun out of control. Mesmo heard the girl call his name frantically as he sped towards the Earth. Everything went black until Mesmo recovered his senses. He saw city lights racing towards him. He tried to veer the spacecraft to the right, only to face a dangerous slope he could not escape.

On the watery screen, Ben and Laura watched as Grampa's house whizzed by, the neon lights from the kitchen, Mr. Hayward's house, the fields and the dark island of trees. Then they saw the explosion as Mesmo's ship hit the ground.

The screen became transparent again. Mesmo let out a gasp of breath as if he had been holding it the whole time. Ben and Laura stared at the alien, speechless.

Ben shivered as Mesmo held his gaze. "Go on," the alien urged.

♦

CHAPTER 11 *The Cosmic Fall*

Reluctantly, Ben touched the liquid mirror again with a trembling hand. In his mind's eye, he was taken back to the field near his grandfather's house.

"There's the Big Dipper," Grampa said, making Ben jump.

Ryan Archer squinted through the eyepiece of an old telescope, which he had directed across the Chilliwack valley and its distant mountains. Grampa and Ben had placed the telescope on top of a blanket in the middle of a nearby field on this starlit August night. A warm breeze brought scents of corn and earth to their nostrils. Trees and shrubs bordered both sides of the field, though to their right they could glimpse the ugly neon light which Grampa had forgotten to switch off when they had set out on their stargazing expedition.

"This was your mother's once, you know?" Grampa said slowly, while he concentrated on getting the image focused. "I made it for her when she was little. Too bad it ended up forgotten in the attic after the lens broke. I'm so glad you found it again!"

He stood to stretch his back, then shook his head. "I can't believe how easy it was to get a new lens delivered to my doorstep! Great job, kiddo!" He patted Ben on the back. "There's a pretty smart brain hiding behind that potatohead of yours!" He chuckled, inviting Ben to check out the stars through the telescope. "I look forward to some more internet surfing classes on your next vacation, eh?"

Ben stuffed the remainder of a biscuit in his mouth, then wiped his hand on his jeans before glancing through the eyepiece. Tike scampered around his feet, bumping into the legs of the telescope.

"Tike!" Ben scolded, his mouth full. His dog kept running around them, barking excitedly.

They followed the dog with their eyes, then noticed what had caught his attention. On the road at the end of the field behind them, Thomas

Nombeko, the friendly town mailman, cycled by on his way home. Thomas waved at them in the dark, shouting something they didn't quite catch.

"'Night, Thomas!" Grampa bellowed, waving back, as the cyclist disappeared into the night. Grampa frowned. "Strange..." he said half to himself. "There's a light on in Mr. Hayward's living room. I thought he was away on business?"

"Grampa! What's that?" Ben shouted, interrupting.

Grampa straightened again, following Ben's pointed finger.

There was a brief, horizontal streak, way up in space, followed by an expanding light as if something had exploded. Then a long, white line descended towards the Earth. It kept falling for what seemed like a long time, its trajectory taking it straight to the lights of Chilliwack.

"Whoa!" Ben gasped in wonder.

But then the falling object did something it wasn't supposed to do; it changed course! What had been a perfectly elliptical line across the black sky, became a soft 90-degree angle, so that without warning, the object was suddenly heading straight towards them.

Shooting stars don't change trajectory! What the heck is going on?

Ben broke into a cold sweat. "Grampa?" his voice wavered.

Grampa gripped the boy's shoulder to pull him away. Instead, they found themselves frozen to the spot. There was nowhere to run, no time to think.

They could hear the burning object whistling through the air as it raced towards them at frightening speed.

"Grampa!" Ben screamed.

Chaos descended upon them with a horrible, screeching noise that went on and on as the object fought its last battle with gravity. They were struck by a deafening explosion, a blinding light, a wave of heat. The ground heaved beneath them.

Tike let out a death howl that pierced Ben's heart. The boy barely registered hitting the ground; the air sucked out of his lungs. Ben and his grandfather lay in a heap, their bodies pelted by dirt bullets.

A heavy silence followed.

The boy extracted his hand from Grampa's tight grip. His brain was rattled. Grampa coughed up dust.

The ball of fire had missed them, landing in the woods nearby. Flames flared behind the dark trees where the object had dragged itself to its terrible end.

Boy and man helped each other stand. Ben found his legs were like jelly. He picked up a silent, shivering Tike in his arms.

"Ben, are you all right?" Grampa asked. He scanned the boy from head to foot, then brushed off some of the dirt on the boy's face.

Ben stared at him with dazed eyes, then nodded slowly.

An object at the edge of the patch of forest caught their eye. They walked towards it slowly, Ben clinging tightly to Grampa's arm. A broken piece had been blown sky-high and had landed on the ground not far from them. It was about the size of a car door, and it had the smooth, silver colour of metal.

"An airplane!" Ben breathed.

That's why it changed course in the middle of the sky!

The poor pilot had managed to veer the ailing aircraft away from a direct crash with the town of Chilliwack in the hopes of finding a place to land. Instead, he had only found a wall of trees in his path.

Grampa took Ben firmly by the arm, pulling him away. They both half-ran, half-trotted across the field in the direction of Grampa's house. They ignored the blanket and telescope. They crossed through the few shrubs and trees separating the two fields and viewed Grampa's house with relief. Ben didn't think the neon kitchen lights could ever look so welcoming. He tugged at his grandfather to get going. Grampa held him back.

"Listen to me very carefully, Benjamin," he said sternly.

Ben listened.

You never call me Benjamin...

"I have to go and help the people who crashed back there."

Ben's mouth opened in a terrified objection.

Grampa held up his hand.

"Boy, time is crucial! I need you to run to the house, pick up the phone and dial 911. Tell the police a plane fell next to my house. We need the fire department and ambulances. Do you understand?"

"No way, Grampa! You're not going back there!" Ben gasped.

"There's no time to argue! Do it, now!" he ordered, his eyes ablaze.

Grampa's words worked like a trigger. A sense of extreme urgency propelled Ben forward. All he could think of were the people who had crashed in the plane.

Ambulance! Fire department!

The words repeated in his mind with each step. His shoes thumped on the dry ground. His eyes fixed on the kitchen light, as it beckoned him. The wide field stretched away from his small frame as he gasped for air. He had almost made it across when something horrifying happened; the lights inside the house went out!

Ben froze. Darkness crashed around him. He could barely make out Grampa's house, now a black, empty giant.

No electricity, no phone...

The realization struck Ben with full force. He picked up Tike in his arms for comfort. The dog shivered uncontrollably.

Drat! Why doesn't Grampa have a cellphone?

The fire in the woods illuminated the sky behind him.

If I hurry, I'll catch up with Grampa.

Ben knew he wasn't thinking straight, but he needed to do something. He couldn't just stand there. The boy bolted away from the house, back across the field, a stitch nagging at his side.

Maybe I can help...

He was too set on finding his grandfather to notice a small burst of light in the night sky, followed by an elliptical line streaking towards the Earth.

Ben was sobbing by the time he reached the blanket and telescope in the middle of the second field. It was a comforting island at the centre of a danger zone. Yet, once there, it was still as cold and lonely, offering no protection. The tears made it impossible to search for Grampa. Everything was a blur.

He sagged down onto the blanket, exhausted and frightened. He wiped away his tears and sniffled.

Stop being a wuss! Grampa needs help.

Feeling ashamed, he blinked several times to clear his eyesight and paid more attention to the wall of dark trees. He took a deep breath, picked up his dog again, then left the blanket and telescope on stiff legs. His whole body ached. The air felt cold and humid, in spite of the crackling fire coming from within the woods.

Ben had nearly reached the edge of the trees when he heard the familiar whistling in the air and caught sight of the fireball out of the corner of his eye. He turned to face it, though he might as well have been a lonely tree about to be swallowed by a tornado. The fiery bullet was already almost on top of him. He barely had time to shut his eyes and brace himself for the impact.

For a second time that night, there was a deafening crash. Ben was knocked to the ground. A heat wave followed, then a grinding hiss that came nearer and nearer. Chunks of earth and metal whizzed by, narrowly missing him. He covered his head with his arms to protect himself and Tike. Heat from the object warmed Ben's face as it came to a stop right before him.

When he opened his eyes, the field resembled a war zone. Huge, twisted pieces of metal surrounded him, burning. A long, fiery runway indicated the distance the object had travelled since its impact. And before him was the craft, or rather what remained of it, for it was almost entirely buried in the ground.

Ben stayed rooted to the spot; his voice stuck in his throat.

The flames licked at the wreckage, minding their own business. Ben stood there, shaking like a leaf before the billowing black smoke. He didn't think the smooth wreckage that jutted out of the ground looked like an airplane at all, though he noticed a hole near the front, indicating it was hollow. Carefully, he took a few steps closer to the opening and glanced inside. He came face to face with a girl. Her big eyes bored into him from deep inside the wreckage. They both froze and stared at each other fearfully.

She had a pale, delicate face and long, white hair. He noticed her eyes were a deep honey-brown before she shut them tightly. She was like a delicate fawn in great pain. Ben knelt on the ground and bent over the opening in the wreckage so he could get a better look. It was dark inside, but the nearby firelight illuminated the girl's face. The rest of her body was stuck under debris.

"Are you hurt?" he asked shakily.

It took a while for her to open her eyes again. When she did, they reflected an immense weariness. Her skin had turned slightly gray.

Ben reached out a hand to her, feeling an urgent need to help. She stared at it suspiciously, showing no intention of taking it. Ben frowned, then suddenly realized his hand was bleeding. He wiped it hastily on his trouser leg, before holding it out to her again. She stared back at his hand, hesitant. At that moment Tike peeked over the edge. As soon as she saw the dog, her expression softened. She turned her face away and he heard her gasp in pain. She looked at him again, with determination this time, as she extended her pale hand to him.

Ben was puzzled to see her palm was

bleeding, too. But before he could say anything, her hand clamped onto his, and instead of bracing herself to get pulled out, she mumbled some unintelligible words while staring at him with an intensity so frightening Ben's heart almost stopped. He tried to pull away, but she had him in an iron grasp. Their eyes locked, their blood smears mingled, and a sudden, powerful surge of energy flowed into Ben's body. His mind exploded in a myriad of sensations as if every stem cell in his brain had been activated.

Then, as suddenly as it had begun, it was over, and she let him go. Ben's arm hung limply over the side of the craft, as he stared down at her in shock. His whole body tingled. Slowly he retrieved his numb arm and found his hand balled into a tight fist. He carefully unwound the fingers of his hand, only to discover a tiny, sparkling gem in its centre.

The diamond in the watch!

Another part of his mind nudged at him, but all he could think of was the girl who gazed at him with a worried look on her face. There was a brief silence as if an electrical storm passed between them. She let herself sink back into the wreckage, her face becoming a deeper gray, her eyes reflecting an inner peace.

"Mesmo," she murmured.

He thought he saw her smile before she closed her eyes.

"No!" Ben shouted, reaching for her as her body slipped out of reach.

Ben's eyes fluttered open. He was back on the beach, sitting before the fire, surrounded by Laura and Mesmo. Before him, the liquid screen had lost its consistency and had splashed to the ground. The embers sizzled. A wind had picked up, while a couple of raindrops fell unnoticed onto the thick sand.

Mesmo breathed heavily, his hand still raised as if he had not yet realized that the watery mirror had disappeared. Ben stared at him with wide eyes.

Laura was the first to come out of her trance. She approached Ben on her knees, taking her son in her arms. "Now I know," she said softly, hugging him.

He squeezed her back, feeling tired and empty, yet also strangely lightheaded, for a great weight had been lifted from his shoulders. Something that had burdened him had suddenly been extracted and was no longer only his to carry. He felt strangely relieved.

Mesmo stood and walked to the edge of the

water. Tiny waves lapped the shore peacefully, though raindrops fell more insistently.

Ben let go of his mother, and walked over to him.

After staring out at the dark waters for a long, silent moment, Mesmo gazed down at Ben quizzically. In a startled voice, he said, "She gave you her skill!"

"What do you mean?" Ben asked as rain splattered down his face.

Mesmo ignored him. He spoke into the night with a broken voice, "Then my daughter truly is dead..."

Laura came up behind them and led Ben away from Mesmo, as the alien continued to stare, motionless, at the black sea. "That's enough for now," she said softly when Ben wanted to object.

Reluctantly, he followed her, sneezing hard. They collected the blankets and empty cans before heading up the steep slope next to the lighthouse. By the time they reached the car, they were worn out. Laura switched on the car heater for a while as they snuggled up as best they could in the car seats, Laura in front and Ben at the back, then covered themselves with their damp jackets. Ben barely recollected his mother switching off the car before he fell into a deep, dreamless sleep.

CHAPTER 12 *The List*

Laura woke to the sound of pounding rain. It washed over the windshield like a waterfall so that she could barely see outside.

She put the key into the ignition without starting the car, revealing the time on the dashboard. Almost 10:30 p.m. Ben stirred in the back seat, so she switched on the radio and tried to make out what the reporter said over the drumming noise outside.

"...Coast Guard has had to call off the rescue mission due to the bad weather conditions and will make another attempt to save the crew of the drifting ship at dawn tomorrow."

A woman took over. "Yes, Ronald, this freak storm will wreak havoc on traffic if it continues tomorrow morning. We urge drivers to be extremely cautious in this treacherous weather, as roads are slippery, with limited visibility..."

Ben stretched and yawned. He glanced around. "Where's Mesmo?"

"I've been wondering the same thing," Laura said. She put on her coat. "I'm going to look for him." She opened the car door, getting soaked as soon as she stepped out.

Ben came up behind her in a hurry. "I'm coming with you!"

You're not closing the door on me again!

They grabbed a blanket, thinking to hold it above their heads. It drenched instantly and stuck like glue to their hair and faces. In the end, they left it, then advanced carefully on the muddy path. They would not have been able to get very far if it hadn't been for the lighthouse that served as a beacon indicating the way.

Soon they saw Mesmo standing upright with his back to them on a flat, rocky ledge, illuminated by the sweeping beam, his elbows close to his body, his hands outstretched, his body glowing faintly from an inner source of energy. As they approached, they saw that not a drop of rain had touched him; he was completely dry and unaffected by the storm raging around him.

Ben and Laura held on to each other to keep from slipping, their hair plastered to their faces, their shoes pools of water.

"Jack!" Laura yelled over the sound of rain. The alien man did not budge. "Mesmo!" she called. "You have to stop this! It won't bring your daughter back. She's gone, Mesmo. There was nothing you could have done. I'm sorry about that. But if you're responsible for this storm, you have to stop immediately! You're putting people in danger. Look around you! We're drowning here!"

She let go of Ben, then reached out to touch Mesmo's shoulder, only to find that there was nothing there! Gasping in surprise, she lost her footing and passed *right through him*!

Ben yelled in fear.

Laura hit the ground, then slid down the smooth, rocky ledge. Only a jutting bush saved her from toppling all the way down into the sea.

"Mom!" Ben cried in horror, rushing to help. On his stomach, he crawled towards her. He stretched out his hand, but she was just out of reach. He looked up at Mesmo's projected image, which stood still, unmoving. The alien's head turned towards them.

"Mesmo!" Ben pleaded. "Help her! Please!"

Ben watched as the solid-looking Mesmo bent to touch the ground. Immediately the rain moved away from them like a curtain. The surface dried up while icy spikes spurted out of the rock all the way down to Laura. She used them to pull herself up. Ben grabbed her, and heaved her up to safety.

They toppled to the ground, breathing heavily, their eyes on Mesmo. The drape of rain fell over them again, though with less intensity.

Woman and child stared at the tall man, unable to comprehend how he could look so real to them. He gazed back, his eyes emitting a million unreadable thoughts. He looked haggard and weak. His skin had turned a light grey.

Then he vanished.

Laura gasped.

She and Ben crawled backwards in fright and stared at the empty spot. The rain continued to fall and the beam from the lighthouse swept by them. Yet they had to accept the unacceptable. Mesmo had disappeared into thin air.

Ben sneezed. Laura helped him up. They trudged back to the car, grasping onto each other as if they might disappear, too. They regularly checked over their shoulders without speaking. Ben sneezed again. They entered the car, soaking wet, and, after a few unsuccessful attempts, Laura started the car. She backed out of the parking space, switched on the lights, and carefully drove away from the haunted lighthouse park.

Ben secretly checked on his mother while she drove.

I can hear you wheezing!

They arrived in North Vancouver where Laura stopped at a Comfort Inn in the hopes of getting a room to shower and rest for the night. There, she found that her credit card was no longer working.

They drove on, shivering with cold. Laura eyed the gas meter nervously. It was dangerously low. It was not easy to find anything open at such a late hour—the streets were empty, especially after such a downpour. They crossed over Highway One and came to an all-night diner called The Bearded Bear. Relieved, they sat down at a table away from late-night truck drivers, and ordered as much food as they could with what little cash Laura managed to fish out of her pocket. While they waited, she insisted on Ben going to the men's room to dry himself off as much as possible. She didn't want him falling sick. She suggested he use the hand dryer on his t-shirt.

I wish I'd brought my suitcase along!

Ben remembered he had left it at school. There was nothing he could do about it now. By the time he came back he felt somewhat refreshed, though his clothes were still damp. The hot food on the table lifted his spirits. A big hamburger awaited, while his mother had ordered chicken soup. He hadn't realized how hungry he was and barely noticed when his mother excused herself to go and clean herself up as well.

He was busy digging into his fries when she came back, but she did not touch her food. He noticed her breath coming out in short bursts. Laura searched through her belongings, telling Ben he could have her soup if he was still hungry.

"Are you sure?" he asked, seriously tempted.

She nodded absentmindedly, going through her things.

"I'll eat your bread roll. But you should have the soup," Ben suggested.

Laura slumped into the high restaurant seat, looking crestfallen. Ben forgot the bread roll he had brought to his mouth. He saw her flushed face.

"What is it, Mom?" he asked, although he had already recognized the signs.

"It's my inhaler," she said with short gasps. She opened her handbag for the third time. "I can't find it! I'm certain I had one, but it's not there anymore."

Ben swallowed the piece of bread which stuck in his throat as he looked at her worriedly.

She tried a small, reassuring smile. "Don't worry, I'll be fine. It's the least of our concerns. Just finish the soup."

"No, Mom, you should eat. You'll feel much better," he insisted.

Laura made an effort to eat, while Ben watched carefully, but soon she put the spoon down and said, "I'm drained, Ben. Could you take care of the bill? There should be enough..." She indicated the money on the table. "I think I'll go and lie down in the car for a bit."

She walked away slowly, while he asked the waitress to pack up the remaining soup and bread to go. By the time he had plopped the coins on the table, counting them twice, his mother was already fast asleep in the back seat. He covered her with the blanket and was going to settle down under her jacket when he noticed an envelope sticking out of its inside pocket.

He opened it and found a small piece of paper that had been torn out of a standard notebook. He recognized his grandfather's handwriting right away. On it, were five names with a phone number under each one.

1. Ryan Archer
   604-721-883
2. Wayne McGuillen
   604-347-222
3. Thomas Nombeko
   250-981-310
4. Susan Pickering
   778-919-832
5. Bob M.
   416-627-003

CHAPTER 13 *The Island*

Ben dozed off while studying the list. He started awake when Tike nuzzled him in the neck. He waved the dog away with his hand, then rested his head uncomfortably against the cold windowpane. The dog jumped onto his lap, placing his two paws on his chest, trying to catch his attention. Ben blinked several times. The lights of the all-night diner were out and the parking lot was empty. Only a couple street lamps produced modest islands of lights, while everything seemed peaceful.

"Go to sleep, Tike," Ben whispered, pushing him away from his face as the dog licked him.

His mother moaned from the back seat. Ben snapped his head in her direction.

Laura tossed in her sleep, the blanket slipping off onto the floor. Ben bent over the car seat to move the locks of hair that were plastered to her cheeks. He touched her hand. It felt cold as ice. She was drenched in sweat and shivering uncontrollably.

She's burning up!

"Mom!" he gasped worriedly.

He covered her with the blanket again, and rolled up his jacket under her head before emptying her purse on the driver's seat in the hopes of finding some analgesic to bring down the fever. He found none. An hour went by and she was worsening. Her breath wheezed again as she twisted on the uncomfortable back seat.

Ben got out of the car and jogged towards the street, searching for a passerby or car. There was no one in sight. He thumped on the door of the diner, knowing full well its occupants had gone. He raked his hands through his hair in despair.

"Mesmo!" he called hesitantly, searching the empty parking lot with his eyes. Only a soft breeze answered.

Tike jumped up to lick his hand encouragingly. They headed back to the car. Ben slipped into the driver's seat. The time on the dashboard said 2:55 a.m. He would have to wait many hours before anybody came along. He glanced at Tike helplessly. The dog sat in the passenger seat, his tongue lolling to one side, with a paw on the sheet of paper that Ben had found in his mother's jacket. Ben fondled the dog's ears while he studied the list of names again.

He knew the first name, Ryan Archer. That was his grandfather. He did not know any of the others. As he stared at the phone numbers again, he realized that the one belonging to Wayne McGuillen started with 604, like his grandfather's, which meant he lived in the same area. He was not familiar with the zone numbers 250 or 416, but he pondered the number that started with 778. That was a local number, he was sure of it. It belonged to someone named Susan Pickering.

He delved into his mother's handbag and pulled out her cellphone, only to realize the battery had died. Desperately, he glanced around and spotted a public phone booth attached to the side of the diner.

I didn't know they still made those!

He had never actually used one before. After going through his jeans pockets, he found he had sufficient coins to make a phone call. He stared into the dark, wondering if this would lead him anywhere.

Tike placed a paw on his arm as if encouraging him to follow his instincts.

"C'mon, Tike," Ben whispered, as he got out of the car and headed for the phone.

He punched the numbers, then listened to the ringing on the other end. It went on and on for some time. He almost gave up, when someone picked up the receiver, and a woman's voice barked, "What?"

Ben was taken aback, then remembered it was three in the morning; decent folk were fast asleep at this time. "Er... hello," he began hesitantly. "Is this Susan Pickering?"

There was a silence. Ben thought she might hang up.

Then the woman said more slowly, "Who wants to know?"

"I... well... my name is Benjamin Archer. I'm Ryan Archer's grandson. I think you knew each other?"

Further silence.

"I'm sorry to bother you, but my mom's very sick, and we need help," he pressed on.

After a while, she said, "Where's Ryan?"

That confirms that they knew each other.

"Grampa died last week. He wrote your

name and phone number on a piece of paper. I thought maybe... well, maybe..." he stammered.

"Where are you?" she interrupted.

Ben glanced around.

I have no idea!

"I don't know exactly... I'm in the parking lot of a place called The Bearded Bear Diner..."

"I know where that is," she said abruptly. "Stay right there! Don't talk to anyone! Don't contact anyone! I'm coming to you." Then she hung up before Ben could say anything else.

The boy stared at the receiver, a million thoughts going through his head. Tike gazed up at him with his tail wagging slowly.

* * *

The waiting was the worst. Ben would sometimes doze off to the strangest of dreams; then he would wake with a start, check on his shivering mother and his surroundings worriedly. It felt like forever before a red car screeched into the parking lot around 5:30 a.m. It came to a stop beside them.

Immediately, a bulky woman with light brown hair worn in a hasty bun on top of her head stepped out, then hurried over to open the driver's door before Ben had time to react. Without a word of greeting, she stared at him with determined, blue eyes. When she noticed Laura lying on the back seat, she checked her vital signs.

"She's running a fever," the woman stated, business-like.

Tell me something I don't know!

She opened the back door of her own car before waving Ben over. "Come on, help me here," she ordered as she began to pull Laura out of the car.

"Wait a minute," Ben protested. "What are you doing? Where are you taking her?"

The woman in her early sixties shot him a stern glance. "You in trouble, boy?"

Ben, taken aback, stared down at his sneakers uncomfortably.

The woman grunted. "Huh! Just what I figured. I'm taking you somewhere safe. You can't very well take her to the hospital, can you?"

Ben silently agreed, though he wished his mother had been conscious enough to approve of what was happening. Reluctantly, he helped the woman carry his mother to the other car.

"Grab your things," Susan urged. She was clearly in a hurry.

Ben did what he was told, though their

belongings were reduced to his mother's handbag, his grandfather's list, and their jackets.

He went to sit beside his mother on the back seat, placing her head to rest on his lap. Tike sat at his feet, trembling with anticipation.

"What about our car?" Ben asked.

Susan Pickering revved up her own red car, speeding away from the parking lot.

"You won't be needing it anymore."

Ben watched as their vehicle disappeared behind the bend.

They drove for about half an hour onto a winding road bordered by sparse houses and areas heavily populated with deep green Douglas firs, until they reached the small town of Deep Cove, nestled at the foot of Mount Seymour and the Burrard Inlet. Rows of sailboats and motorboats were anchored in the marina. As dawn approached, Ben could make out the outline of the mountains on the other side of the inlet and dark, sporadic islands jutting from the water.

Susan Pickering turned left off the marina, driving until the houses became less frequent. Then she abruptly took a small dirt road to the right, which soon led to a run-down shed and small, wooden pier by the water. She got out of the car, then busied herself opening the shed door and foraged inside.

Ben stepped out of the car as well, taking in his surroundings. The calm waters turned a lighter shade of blues and pinks as the sun began to rise, contrasting with last night's storm.

Susan Pickering had found some blankets in the shed, which she carried to a small motorboat tied to the end of the pier.

"Are we taking the boat?" Ben asked nervously.

"Sure are," the woman answered. "Give me a minute."

She disappeared back into the shed, leaving Ben with his stomach churning. He did not like the idea of open water. He wrapped his arms around his shoulders as if to warm himself, feeling his grandfather's watch close to his cheek. Suddenly Tike ran behind Ben excitedly. The boy whirled, and jumped at the sight of Mesmo standing only a few feet away. Ben stepped back, unsure what to expect, as he stared at the imposing man.

"What happened?" Mesmo asked, seeing the shed, the boat, then Laura, lying in the back seat of the car.

"She's very sick," Ben said weakly, wondering which direction he should run if it became necessary. But the alien cut off any escape to the winding road they had used, while the open waters trapped him from behind.

I can't leave Mom behind!

Mesmo had not moved since he had magically appeared, so Ben mustered up enough courage to approach him. He reached out his hand. Mesmo understood his gesture and did the same. Ben waved his hand up and down, each time going right through Mesmo's own.

Ben stepped back, asking with a shaky voice, "Are you a ghost?"

Mesmo's eyes twinkled as if he found the question funny. "A ghost is a spirit belonging to someone whose body has died," he began. "I am not a ghost. My body is not dead. It is just not... here right now." He paused, before adding, "But my spirit is free to roam."

Behind them, Susan Pickering, who had emerged from the shed, stopped in her tracks. "What...!" she began. "Who's that?" Her face flushed with anger.

Ben held up his hands to calm her down. "It's okay! He's a friend!"

She stepped closer to take a better look at the stranger. The fact that a lock of white hair stuck out from under Mesmo's fur hat made him look quite out of place.

"He's a friend," Ben repeated, trying to sound reassuring. "His name is Mes... er... his name is Jack Anderson. He's..."

Susan Pickering interrupted him. "I know who he is," she snorted. She had her hands on her hips, inspecting the man up and down like he was some curious object. After a while, she said sternly, "You've caused a lot of harm, Mister. A lot of harm." She shook her head disapprovingly. "How did you find us anyway?"

Ben cleared his throat to come to the rescue. "Er... he was following us. Didn't you notice?"

Susan Pickering frowned at him angrily. "Was he now?" Then she sighed, adding, "Well, I don't want to know. But since you're here, might as well prove yourself useful. Help me carry this sick lady into the boat, would you?"

Ben and Mesmo shot a glance at each other. The boy ran to Susan's side, blurting, "I can help!"

Ben and Susan struggled to pull a very weak Laura out of the car, then the three of them stumbled down to the pier while Mesmo watched from a distance. With some difficulty, they managed to place Laura on the back seat of the motorboat. Susan went back to her car to drive it into the shed, then closed and locked the door with a padlock.

They all took a seat in the boat. Susan, who saw that Mesmo was not helping her by uncoupling the rope that held the boat to the pier, grumbled, "Men!" under her breath, before bringing the motorboat to life. Ben had to bite his lip to stop himself from grinning, while Mesmo stared at him in bewilderment.

They headed off into the inlet, a bright, cold sun chasing away the night and the remaining clouds from last night's storm. In spite of the low temperature, it was going to be a beautiful day. Susan had provided some thick blankets to keep Laura warm, which Ben struggled to keep in place as the wind tried to blow them away. All the while he couldn't help gawking at Mesmo.

Jeepers! This guy is some kind of phantom from outer space!

He fought off the urge to laugh crazily and forgot that the sky had been weighing down on his shoulders only moments ago.

They sped past one of the small islands, then approached another. Ben made sure he was out of earshot before mustering up the courage to sit near the alien, making sure not to touch him. He asked, "What is it like, where you come from?"

Mesmo didn't seem to mind the question.

"It's not that much different from this place," he replied as he indicated the calm waters and surrounding mountains. "What I mean is, you'd have to fly at a very low altitude to realize that there was a whole city spread out under the forests, hills and snowy mountains. It is a very beautiful and... balanced... place. We have many laws to maintain this balance, we grow up with the deepest respect for them. Which is also why we do not have wars or hunger or suffering because we do not allow ourselves to experience strong, conflicting emotions like people on your planet."

He blinked as if realizing that Ben was wondering where all this was going. He cleared his throat, then continued, "Our lifespans are longer than Earth humans by about forty years. We have three suns and four moons. Our days last thirty-two hours. We have cities on the moons and in the oceans. We live where our skills are most useful. Our skills give us purpose in life."

Intrigued, Ben wanted to ask more questions, but Susan had turned around, gesturing for him to grab onto the rope. They were already slowing to a stop next to the wooden pier of a tree-filled island in the middle of the inlet.

The chubby woman deftly maneuvered the motorboat next to another rustier one, which also lay docked there. A large patch of grass led to a fringe of tall fir trees. Ben could make out the shape of a log cabin tucked between them. It was quaint and inconspicuous.

The perfect hiding place!

"Where are we?" Ben asked.

"Home," Susan replied.

"Oh..." Ben nodded, understanding why it had taken her so long to pick them up from The Bearded Bear Diner.

With some effort, Susan and Ben managed to help Laura out of the boat. They dragged her to the cabin, with Susan muttering under her breath the whole way because Mesmo deliberately lagged behind. Ben had to suppress a nervous giggle again. If this woman found out that Mesmo wasn't really there, but was some illusion or projected image, she would kick them into the inlet in a heartbeat!

The cabin was surprisingly cozy. On the left was a small, functional kitchen with a white, countertop island, while on the right, a snug living room with an open fireplace. The walls and roof were made of logs, the floor was planked with wooden boards. Some sustaining logs crisscrossed the ceiling. Practically everything Ben laid his eyes on was made of wood, which gave the whole place a warm, camping-out-in-the-forest sort of feeling.

Further in, Ben glimpsed a wooden dining table with four chairs, as Susan directed him through a door at the end of the living room which led to a bedroom with a large, thick mattress on an old bed frame. They placed Laura on top of it, and she moaned as she sank into the soft, plush duvet.

No sooner was this done than Susan shooed Ben out of the room, ordering him to get the rest of the things from the boat. She did, however, allow Tike to stay quietly on the bed next to Laura. Ben did as he was told, then found he had nothing more to do but sit restlessly in the living room with Mesmo. An old cuckoo clock ticked loudly while they waited.

Ben was glad to get another chance to interrogate the alien. "Where did you go last night?" he asked.

Mesmo did not reply right away, as if pondering how much he should say. "Spirit travelling takes a lot of energy and concentration. Sometimes it is necessary for me to return to my physical body to regain strength."

Ben could tell that there was more to it than that, but since Mesmo offered no further explanation, he asked, "What about what you did with the rain puddle in the parking lot? And the boiling water? And the ice spikes on the rock? Those were real!" Ben insisted.

Mesmo nodded. "My skill is not connected to my body. It is connected to my spirit. I take my skill with me when my spirit travels."

"You keep on talking about your skill. And last night you said 'She gave you her skill.' What did you mean by that?" Ben asked.

Mesmo stared at him intently.

"My skill is *water*," he began carefully. "I can manipulate it in any way I choose. It's a very useful tool on this planet and one of the reasons I was chosen for this mission. Bordock's skill is *shapeshifting*. He can take on the shape of any being, though at a great cost in energy. Kaia—my daughter—her skill was... how would you say..." He searched for the word. "My daughter's skill was *translation*. I was against her coming, but she knew how important she was to the mission. She would not back down." His voice trailed off as he remembered.

"Translation...?" Ben asked carefully, eager for an explanation.

Mesmo ignored him and continued. "Bordock wanted to exterminate us, along with our skills, so we would not be able to complete our mission." He stopped. "I don't think he counted on my daughter leaving her skill with you."

Ben felt a chill run down his spine.

I don't want to talk about Bordock!

"Wait a minute. You said your daughter's skill was translation. What does that mean?"

Mesmo searched for his words again. "Well, it's when you understand different languages and can pass on meaning from one language to another so that different beings can communicate with each other."

Ben was utterly perplexed. "That doesn't make sense. I don't speak French or understand Japanese or anything like that."

Mesmo looked at him, amused, before answering. "Maybe not human languages. But languages from different species."

Ben continued to stare at him, confused.

Mesmo added, "Those dogs who attacked Bordock in the parking lot—they understood you, didn't they?"

CHAPTER 14 *Spirit Portal*

Ben sat opposite Mesmo in Susan Pickering's living room, his mind bubbling with questions. Unfortunately, he did not get a chance to interrogate the alien further, as Susan appeared in the bedroom doorway. She glanced at them before busying herself in the kitchen. Within minutes she produced a peanut butter sandwich, which Ben accepted gratefully, although at this point he was having a hard time keeping his eyes open.

"How is she?" Mesmo asked. Through a yawn, Ben still couldn't understand how the alien could look so real.

"Her fever is high," Susan stated, as she poured water into a kettle, then placed it on the stove. "I've given her something to bring down the temperature. All we can do is make her comfortable and wait for her immune system to kick in. Could be a couple of days."

"What about her asthma?" Ben blurted, his brain functioning in a haze.

Susan glanced at him hastily. "Asthma?" When he nodded, she said, "What are you talking about, son?"

"Last night," he began, searching his memory, "she was looking for her asthma pump and couldn't find it."

Out of the corner of his eye, Ben caught the worried look that crossed Susan's face.

"What?" he asked fearfully. "We can get another one from the pharmacy, right?"

Susan answered carefully. "We'll see what we can do. Right now, young man, you're going to take a hot shower and change out of those smelly clothes so I can give them a good wash." She motioned for Ben to follow her up the stairs, where there was another big bedroom and bathroom across the narrow hall.

"But," Ben objected, following her. "I don't have anything else to wear."

"Here," she said, throwing a large, light blue shirt at him. It was obviously hers, so Ben blushed.

Susan saw the look on his face, then scolded, "Come, there's no one else here. You think he cares?" She gestured down at Mesmo who was still in the kitchen observing the boiling water in the kettle. "Towels are in the bathroom," she added, heading down again.

"Wait!" Ben called after her. She stopped midstride. "I still don't know who you are! I mean, why are you helping us?"

She turned back to face him. "I'm a witness, like you." She said, staring meaningfully at him. "I had a small cabin in the woods in Chilliwack, not far from your grandfather's house. Used to go there whenever I could, to clear my mind. I was a nurse at the Children's Hospital, you see. Tough place." She paused. "I was in my cabin, on the night of *The Cosmic Fall*. I heard the explosions in the forest, called 911, then ran with my first aid kit to see if anyone was injured."

She looked down at Mesmo, "That's when I saw you, your... 'companion'... and the spaceships... I knew instinctively I wasn't supposed to be there. Ran back to my cabin as though the hounds of hell were after me! I was terrified, I don't mind saying. Didn't take long for the helicopters and police to arrive. Then later the military. The area turned into a war zone! They brought me in for questioning, along with other witnesses, including your grandfather."

She stayed lost in thought for a while. "I guess they thought we might have been in collusion with the aliens, or infected with some extraterrestrial disease, or, worse still, that we were actually little green men in disguise..." Her voice raised in anger as she spoke, so she sucked in air to calm down, then added, "Let's just say your grandfather was a very resourceful man. He managed to contact the Human Rights Commission, and suddenly we were released, a full three weeks later, when the news had died down at last! We thought we were free, but the police watched our every move like hawks. They bugged our phones. I even found hidden cameras in my elder son's home. They were so afraid we would talk. It was because of the Chinese and the Americans, you see. They're all involved in this, they all want to know the truth..."

She glared down at Mesmo. "Anyway, to make a long story short, Ryan Archer offered me a chance to slip away and lay low for a while, away from prying eyes. So I took it, even though it meant not seeing my sons again." After a silence, she finished, "I've been living here ever since."

She headed down the stairs. "I know you

were there, too, Ben. Fortunately for you, they never found out. Your grandfather made sure of that. He made me promise, if you were ever in trouble, to help you. So that's what I'm doing."

* * *

Ben couldn't remember falling asleep. When he opened his eyes, he was snug in bed in the upstairs room. After listening for sounds and not hearing anything, he tiptoed downstairs. He checked in with his mother, finding her fast asleep, with Tike stretched out next to her, guarding her. The dog opened a sleepy eye, then hopped off the bed excitedly. He rolled on the living-room floor happily, expecting a tummy rub, which Ben obliged to. Tike then pulled at Susan's large t-shirt playfully.

"Are you laughing at me?" Ben teased, chasing after the dog. He headed to the kitchen, grabbed an apple and was taking a bite when he saw the note. "Getting groceries. Your clothes are in the dryer. Susan."

Ben peeked outside, realizing it was still light. While munching on the apple, he found the dryer with his and his mother's clothes clean and warm inside. He pulled on his jeans, the apple caught between his teeth, then folded his mother's clothes as best he could before placing them on her bed. He stood by her side for a while, noticing that her breathing was short. He wiped her face gently with a cold, wet cloth, then stroked her hand. She did not wake up. He roamed in and out of the house looking for Mesmo, Tike at his heels, but the alien was nowhere to be seen.

Susan came back around 4 p.m., the motorboat full of groceries. She put him to work, carrying bags, putting away food in the fridge, boiling water in the kettle, making tea, cutting vegetables and setting the table. Although the woman was bossy, Ben was happy for the distraction.

Soon the house smelled of hot vegetable soup and oven-baked chicken with mushrooms. Ben's stomach rumbled. Susan made a tray with fresh bread, soup, some chicken and tea, which she brought to Laura's bedside. With difficulty, they managed to prop up her head on a thick pillow so she could take a couple sips. She was so frail that she could not handle the bread or chicken. She tried to give Ben a reassuring smile, though the dark circles around her eyes told another story.

Susan and Ben sat down for supper silently.

Digging hungrily into his food, Ben asked, "Were you able to get her inhaler? I couldn't find it in the grocery bags."

Susan glanced at him. "No, son. Asthma inhalers require a doctor's prescription, which we can't get at the moment."

Ben's shoulders drooped as he stared at his soup.

"She'll be fine," Susan said sternly. "Let her fight this. She's strong enough." She must have noticed he wasn't convinced, because she added, "Asthma inhalers aren't a cure for influenza, son." She gestured towards his plate. "Eat! It won't do her any good if you fall sick too."

Her words stuck in his mind, so he forced himself to eat, even though his throat was tight. He noted that she did not ask about Mesmo or why he wasn't around anymore.

* * *

On the third day, Laura's fever still had not broken and her skin was whiter than the bedsheets. Susan watched her until deep into the night. Ben took over during the day while Susan tried to catch up on sleep, but the truth was Ben was not sleeping much either. He was beside himself with worry. He had already tried to convince Susan several times to take his mother to the doctor. She tried to reassure him, telling him that she was monitoring Laura's temperature closely, and reminding him that going to a doctor or hospital was too risky.

Ben sulked at the edge of the water where he sat down, staring dismally at his feet as they dangled from the pier. He touched his watch unconsciously.

Grampa, I wish you were here...

He was so deep in thought that he did not notice Mesmo poised on the lawn, gazing out at sea, his face turned towards the sunshine, like a flower that had been placed in the shadow for too long. Tike went to greet him, inviting him down to the pier. The tall man followed the dog, then bent down next to Ben. The boy sniffled and wiped his eyes as he turned away. Then he said angrily, "Where have you been?"

Mesmo rested his arms on his knees. "I told you," he began carefully. "I can't be away from my physical body for too long."

"Well, why don't you bring your body over here next time?" Ben snapped.

"It's not that simple," Mesmo said.

"I don't get it," Ben insisted. "Why are you

here sometimes, and sometimes you're not?"

Mesmo replied gently, "That kind of depends on you."

Ben stared at him, confused, then saw that Mesmo was pointing at his wristwatch. "Do you remember when Kaia gave this to you?" Mesmo asked, indicating the tiny, glittering gem at the centre of the watch. "I guess your grandfather had it placed in this watch for you. You used it unknowingly for the first time a couple of weeks ago. I was in South America then. I felt it call me. I thought it was Kaia! I immediately boarded a plane to Toronto by using the identity of Jack Anderson." He paused, gazing into the distance. "I had hoped that, somehow, Kaia had survived and was calling to me. That was the only logical explanation. Then I reached your grandfather's funeral, and found out it was you, all along..."

He fell silent, so Ben had to push him on. "Me, all along, who did... what?"

Mesmo looked at him with his honey-coloured eyes, "...you, who was calling me..." He pointed at the watch again. "...with this."

They both stared at the shimmering diamond-like stone.

Mesmo explained, "You could call it a spirit portal. It's a device that, when activated, allows my spirit to travel to it. When you touch the device and call me with your mind, I will hear the call and can then decide whether or not I wish to travel to you in spirit. A human from Earth could not activate it, but I guess you are more than a normal Earth human now..."

Ben decided to ignore a quiver in the pit of his stomach and studied the shiny gem instead. "I'm glad you're here," he said. "My mom's not getting any better. I know she needs her asthma pump. I'm sure she has a spare one at home. All we need to do is sneak into the apartment. I know where she would have kept it..."

Mesmo held up his hand. "Ben, listen to me." His eyes were unreadable as he said slowly, "I came to tell you that I can help you no further."

Ben shook his head as if to get rid of his words. "No, it's okay. I've got it all figured out. You see all we have to do is..."

"Ben!" Mesmo interrupted. The boy stopped in mid-sentence with his mouth open. Mesmo repeated more insistently, "I only came to make sure that you were safe. But I can't help you any longer."

Ben stared at him, incredulous. "Yes, you can! Of course, you can. You've got all those powers. You've helped before. Why wouldn't you help us now?"

When the white-haired man answered by remaining silent, Ben stood up hastily, casting him a furious look. "Well, go on then!" he yelled, tears flowing down his cheeks. "Do your disappearing trick! You're so good at that! See if I care! My mom and I, we've gotten by fine without you before. It's not like we need you now!"

He ran to the cabin, Tike close at his heels, ignoring Susan who had been observing them from afar. She dried her hands on her apron, glaring at Mesmo, before heading back inside.

* * *

That night Ben snuck into bed early without talking to anyone.

Susan finished cleaning up the kitchen when she noticed Mesmo in the doorway, looking out. She joined him, then stopped in her tracks, for she quickly realized what had attracted his attention.

Like a ghost in the moonlight, a huge, white moose stood quite still, close by the water. The skin from this proud, adult male glittered from the long swim it had just taken. Its large antlers crowned its head while steam came from his nostrils. Susan stared in awe as she stood silently beside Mesmo. "I'd heard of them—these albino moose. They are extremely rare," she breathed, afraid to startle the animal. "I never thought I'd see one up close." She glanced at the white-haired alien beside her, taken aback by the meaning of her own words. They observed the beast until it faded away into the nearby trees.

Susan Pickering stared up at Mesmo giddily, her voice coming in a whisper, "Did you make it come?"

Mesmo shook his head, "No. It wasn't me. It was the boy."

Susan started. "Ben? How? I thought he was..."

"...human?" Mesmo finished for her. "Yes, he is human. But my daughter passed on her skill to him. She passed on her ability to communicate with other species. He just isn't aware he's doing it. The moose must have sensed something, and couldn't figure out what it was."

Susan remained silent, pondering this information. After a while, she asked carefully, "What are you doing here, Jack?"

"Mesmo," he corrected. "My name is Mesmo."

"All right, Mesmo," she repeated. "What are you doing here, exactly?"

He stared at her for a moment, before answering, "Why do you ask, Susan Pickering? The less you know, the less trouble you will attract to yourself. I know you know that." He let his comment hang, before offering, "My task is to be an observer. My companions were going to help me complete this mission, but now that they are dead, I am not sure I will make it..."

Susan shook her head to indicate she did not want to hear any more. "No, no," she argued. "That's not what I meant. I wasn't asking you what you're doing here, on Earth. I don't want to know about those things. I'm asking what you're doing here, on my island, in my cabin."

Mesmo shifted, showing unease at her question. Then he reached out a hand towards her. "Take my hand."

She frowned suspiciously, wondering where this was going, then hesitantly lifted her hand to take his. Instead of touching real, solid flesh and bone, her hand slid right through his, as though it were made of thin air. She jumped back, holding on to her hand as if it had been burnt.

Mesmo gave her a small smile. Before she could find her voice, he said, "No. I am not a ghost."

He gazed out at the night while Susan

remained stuck to the wall, afraid to move an inch. "I can disconnect my spirit from my body and travel great distances in the blink of an eye. However, to do so, I must have access to a portal which will allow me to appear as you see me now." He paused. "The boy has that portal."

He turned to face her again, his eyes hidden under the shadows of his brow. "You see, I fell into a trap at the Toronto Airport. I was lured into a corridor away from other travellers. Several men attacked me, knocking me unconscious. When I woke up, I was strapped to a bed in a white room surrounded by machines and men in doctor's coats. I do not know who is holding me or why. But they know who I am and that I am not from this planet."

He spoke with a strain in his voice, "My people respect freedom above all. We do not do well in confined spaces. Being shut away from the outside kills us. If the boy had not activated the spirit portal, thus offering me a means of escape— even though it is only an illusion of sorts—my situation would have become unbearable. I would have died long ago." He stared at Susan before finishing, "I am here, on your island, Susan Pickering, because the boy is keeping me alive..."

Susan regained her composure, the fear in

her eyes slowly replaced by displeasure as he spoke. "So it's exactly as I thought," she muttered.

Mesmo stared at her blankly.

She approached him, pointing an accusing finger, though from a safe distance to avoid touching his non-essence. "You're not here *for* the boy; you're here *because* of him," she hissed.

Mesmo shook his head, not understanding. "Is there a difference?"

"There's a huge difference," she said sternly. "The boy thinks you care about him, that you're here for him. You're not, you're only using him to survive." Since he didn't react, she continued, "You're torturing that boy! He's forming a bond with you; he looks up to you. The longer you stay, the harder it will be for him to see you go. Because, one day, you will go. Or am I wrong?"

When Mesmo still didn't reply, she sighed, exasperated at his seeming lack of understanding. "Don't you see? If his mother dies, he'll be on his own..."

They heard a clatter as someone closed the upstairs bedroom window. Susan glared at Mesmo angrily. She knew Ben had overheard their whole conversation.

The alien's eyes were shrouded in the dark, his face expressionless. "Yes, Susan Pickering, I am using the boy to stay alive, as you say, and, yes, I will leave when I am done here. Where I come from, we do not give in to strong emotions the way humans do. I must remain neutral and impartial if I am to complete my mission..."

"Neutral and impartial!" Susan snorted. "You stopped being neutral and impartial the minute you fell from the sky! The minute you lost your daughter and met them." She pointed indoors to show she was referring to Ben and Laura. She stepped into the cabin, away from the cold. "You call yourself an observer. Well, my alien friend, I think it's time you opened your eyes."

* * *

Mesmo gazed at the stars for a long moment, thinking of Susan's words, for they resonated in his mind like an echo. Had his friend Amaru not said something very similar recently, on the high Andes Mountains of Bolivia? Something about having lost his ability to be the Observer? He struggled with this thought before Kaia's beautiful face emerged in his memories, and he knew he must continue, no matter what. For her sake.

He stepped inside, then headed to the

bedroom where Laura was fighting for her life. Her body was shivering. Her forehead glistened with sweat. Though he could not physically touch her, he could sense the water imbalance in her body as his hand hovered over her shoulder. He concentrated for a moment, sending a warm flow of energy from his palms into her body until the balance had somewhat been restored. She stopped shivering and rested more peacefully. He could not heal her, but at least she would be calm for a while.

Mesmo noticed how her hair had turned a dull, lifeless colour. It was a sharp contrast with the subtle halo of light that had formed around the contour of her head as the setting sun had shone through her ash blonde hair back on the fields of Chilliwack. Her green eyes had stood out against the early autumn pallet of ginger, apricot and maroon-coloured leaves. He traced her fine features into his mind, closed his eyes, then let himself glide back to his physical body, which lay almost three thousand miles away.

As usual, he first recovered his hearing, which captured the low beeping of machines, then he opened his eyes to blurry, artificial light, and, lastly, he felt the pain. It always hit him like a brick wall, making him groan. Even though he knew to expect it, he could not get used to it.

Immediately, he heard the muffled voices of several men who rushed into the room in their pale green antiviral, protective suits and mouth covers.

One of them waved a bright light into Mesmo's eyes, confirming, "He's back." While another ordered, "Check his vital signs." A third one was pulling at the straps that pinned his arms and legs to the hospital bed.

"He's good," the second one said, after analyzing a heart monitor.

"Call the boss," the first voice ordered through the only doorway leading out of the white, bleached room. "Tell him he's back. Vital signs have returned to normal."

The third man injected something into Mesmo's arm, muttering, "Where'd our Martian go this time, I wonder?"

CHAPTER 15 *The Crossing*

Inspector James Hao and Agent Theodore Connelly met in the hallway of the Vancouver Police Department.

Hao quizzed, "Well?" As they entered an elevator going up to the fifth floor.

Connelly reported, "Still nothing. All we have is Laura Archer's attempt to register at the Comfort Inn in North Vancouver and the abandoned car at The Bearded Bear Diner. We've interrogated all possible witnesses. We've gone through all local traffic video cameras. We've found nothing. Not a trace of them."

The elevator pinged when they arrived. They stepped out, headed down the corridor, then into an office with a desk strewn with documents.

Hao searched through the papers, before pulling out a file.

Connelly said, "We have no reports from any units placed in the area. That guy you saw with Laura Archer outside the notary office in Chilliwack might still be helping them. We don't know who he was."

Hao growled, "Well, if you had actually been there instead of running off on your own wild-goose-chase, maybe we wouldn't be asking ourselves that question!" He licked the tip of his finger to flip through the file as he glared at his partner.

Connelly's mouth twitched.

Turning his attention to the file again, Hao said thoughtfully, "We know they are running out of money since we froze Laura Archer's accounts. Plus the waitress from the diner said the boy paid for their food with change. We also know they no longer have a car. So they can't be far. We have units controlling all major exits. They will have to come out in the open sometime." He pointed at the report. "The waitress said Laura Archer didn't eat, then left the boy alone to pay. Why did she do that?"

Connelly shrugged. "How should I know? What do we do now? We have no other leads... "

Hao put down the report, smiling. "Oh, I think we do. It's only a matter of time."

* * *

Ben tiptoed down the stairs in the dark. He was fully dressed. It was not yet dawn, and a chill made it through his sweatshirt. He borrowed a plaid blanket which he put over his shoulders to ward off the cold. Silently, he peeked into the bedroom where his mother lay.

Ben took his mother's hand, whispering, "Hang in there, Mom. I'll be back soon."

He gestured to Tike, who jumped happily into his arms, then the boy grabbed the boat key that hung next to the front door. The two of them ran swiftly to the pier where they hopped into one of the motorboats. Although fog clung to the water, Ben could make out the lights from Deep Cove and the outline of the mountains, as dawn neared.

The boy released the boat from the pier, then took an oar to maneuver it away from the shore. Once he was at a safe distance, he put the key into the ignition, then, his heart beating fast, switched the motor to life. It made a huge racket in the silent night. He looked around fearfully, certain he would wake up half the inlet. Everything remained peaceful, so he moved the motorboat forward slowly, his hands trembling as he learned to control it. He had to stretch his neck to get a good view over the front of the vessel, though in the end, it turned out to be quite manageable.

He was making good way when the mist cleared slightly, revealing a navy blue sky with some twinkling stars above. The pitch dark waters surrounded him, while the night sky went on and on into the void overhead. Although he had left the island several minutes ago, his heart still beat fast. He wiped his forehead with the back of his hand and found it glistening with sweat in spite of the cold air. His breath came in gasps.

What's wrong with me?

With dread, he recognized the symptoms, but it was too late. The sky collapsed on him from all sides. His vision blurred. In a desperate move, he switched off the motorboat before dropping to his knees with his hands to his head. The vast, empty night swallowed him up, crushing him to the floor of the swaying boat.

He had a clear vision of himself standing in the field next to his grandfather, listening to the hissing noise just before the spaceship came crashing to Earth. Everything swayed, making him feel physically sick.

"Grampa! Grampa!" Ben begged.

Tike jumped up and down before him with his ears laid back, trying to pull the boy out of the panic attack that had grasped his mind.

"Ben!" Grampa called, as he stood silhouetted against the burning wreck.

"Ben!"

The boy heard his name loud and clear, except it wasn't coming from his mind, but rather from the boat he was crouching in. He opened his eyes carefully, trying to comprehend how Grampa could have materialized onto the boat with him.

Mesmo stared at him from the back of the boat. The alien called his name; his hand plunged into the water as if he were testing its temperature.

Ben slowly uncurled his arms from his head. He noticed the boat was no longer rocking about aimlessly, instead, it felt stable as it advanced at a slow pace. He stood up carefully, his mind clearing. Behind Mesmo, the town of Deep Cove slowly receded. He turned to face the front of the boat. His eyes widened as he realized it was heading back towards the island at a steady pace.

"No! Stop that! You're going the wrong way!"

Mesmo scolded, "It's too dangerous! You

can't do this on your own!"

Ben's eyes welled with tears. "What am I supposed to do then, huh? Who's going to go with me?" He glared at Mesmo. "Are you?"

Mesmo stared at him intently without answering.

"Exactly!" Ben continued. "You're not going to do anything about it! So go away! Mind your own business!"

"Benjamin!" Mesmo said sternly. "I need your help." He lifted his hand out of the water. Immediately the boat began to rock softly to-and-fro.

Ben's jaw dropped. "*You* need *my* help?" He stared, incredulous. "Is that supposed to be a joke?" He turned his head away, not wanting Mesmo to see the hurt on his face. Before he thought better of it, he snapped, "Why didn't you say anything before? About being kidnapped?"

Mesmo answered, "My problems did not concern you. I had expected to get out of this mess already. But I have no access to water, so I can't defend myself." He wrung his hands together, saying in defeat, "I don't think I can get out."

Ben stared at the sea, a mixture of emotions bubbling inside him. "So, am I supposed to feel sorry for you now?" he snapped.

"No." Mesmo answered matter-of-factly. "But I want you to understand why I said I am no longer able to help you. My abilities are limited. If you cross this inlet to try to get your mother's medication on your own, I can't guarantee that I will be there to help you. You need to go back to the island and find a solution with the Pickering woman."

"I don't have time to sit around and chat with Susan!" Ben retorted. "I might be too late already!" He sat down heavily, pulling the plaid blanket around him. He hung his head between his knees, sulking.

After a long silence, Ben peeked over his arm, suddenly afraid that Mesmo was gone. But the alien had his head turned towards the stars, as though he were drinking in the fading night with his whole being. He closed his eyes as the first ray of sunlight cut through the horizon.

Ben couldn't help noticing how Mesmo's skin tone went from a light grey to a darker, healthier tan. "Why didn't you tell me I was keeping you alive?" he muttered.

He didn't think Mesmo had heard him, but the alien opened his dark eyes. "It wasn't your burden to carry."

Alien and boy stared at each other as a bright sun emerged between patches of thick clouds.

Ben said, "Look. You need me. I need you. Help me get my mother's inhaler. Then we will help you out from wherever you are. Once we've freed you, you can go on with your precious mission, and my mom and I can go home."

The white-haired man gazed thoughtfully at the boy, before stating carefully, "I don't think..." He suddenly grimaced and bent over in pain, surprising Ben.

"What's the matter?" Ben said quickly, but only the soft morning breeze blew over the boat in answer. Mesmo was already gone. Ben sat down again, disheartened. "Come back," he begged to the wind.

* * *

After waiting in vain for Mesmo to return, Ben sighed, then said to his terrier, "It's just you and me, Tike."

He pondered the island for a while.

Should I go back?

Tike placed a paw on his leg encouragingly.

"I can't face Mom with empty hands, can I?" He took a deep breath, turned on the motor, and navigated the boat towards Deep Cove again. He had enough worries on his mind this time to remember he was actually supposed to be afraid of the open skies. Somehow Mesmo's presence had pushed away all thoughts of panic attacks. As he attached the boat to the pier of the quaint harbour, he breathed in deeply with renewed energy.

He and Tike jogged to the nearest bus stop where they took the first bus to the Lonsdale Quay in North Vancouver. There, they hopped onto the Seabus that crossed the short sea arm to the City of Vancouver. Ben and Tike hopped onto the Skytrain heading to Burnaby, where he reached his apartment block. It felt like an eternity since he had last seen the low-lying, three-story building with twelve apartments.

The boy hesitated, knowing there could be danger. He hid behind some bushes on the other side of the street, carefully scanning the area. Five minutes later a police officer walked out of the building, got into a police car, and drove away.

"We're in luck!" Ben whispered to Tike. He ran across the road to the back of the building, carefully making his way to the end until he was right below his own bedroom window.

"Wait here, Tike," he ordered. The dog sat

down obediently.

Nimbly, Ben grabbed onto the drainpipe, climbed onto the windowsill of the downstairs neighbour, and checked no one was inside. He pulled himself up until he reached his window. It opened smoothly as the lock had broken many years ago and had never been fixed. Swiftly, he dropped into his bedroom and looked out the window, making sure no one had seen him. Only Tike stared up at him, tail wagging and tongue lolling.

Ben scanned his messy bedroom. He hopped across the room, avoiding a dirty plate, his Xbox controller, a bicycle helmet, and comic books. He failed to notice a football hiding under the hanging sheets of his bed. He kicked it accidentally with his foot. It rolled across the room and struck the door with a thud. Ben froze and listened for any noise coming from the apartment. All he heard was his thumping heart. He let out his breath in relief.

He grabbed an old backpack and stuffed underwear, socks, trousers and shirts into it. Next, he crept across the hallway into his mother's room, scanned it for any danger, and packed some clothing for her as well. He opened all the drawers hurriedly, searching for an extra asthma inhaler his mother might have kept tucked away. He found nothing.

Once the backpack couldn't hold another thing, he closed the zip, placed it on his shoulders, and left the bedroom to continue his search. A movement at the end of his mother's bedroom made him jump before he realized it was only his reflection in a mirror. He wanted to kick himself.

Pull yourself together!

He stepped into the corridor.

The man with black hair streaked with grey stood at the other end of it, waiting for him. He held up an asthma inhaler. "Looking for this?" the man taunted.

Ben's heart sank like a stone. He recognized the neatly dressed man from the funeral reception he had found handling his grandfather's telescope.

The man took out a badge with a picture ID. "James Hao," he said, presenting himself again. "*Inspector* James Hao, from the Canadian Security Intelligence Service. I thought you might be needing this at some point." He waved the inhaler at Ben before putting it into his trouser pocket. "I think you and I need to have that chat now."

Not on your life!

Ben rushed into the bathroom, shut the door, and locked it. Not a split moment later Hao banged against it, shouting, "Open up!"

Ben heard him call for reinforcements. He opened the bathroom window and threw the backpack out, narrowly missing Tike below. Ben had a leg out the window when he looked back, struck by a sudden idea. He jumped back into the bathroom and opened the drawers, frantically searching through the brushes, toothpaste, hair dryer and makeup.

At the very back, in a corner, he found something he hadn't expected to find but took anyway. It was his mother's engagement ring—the one Ben's dad had given her before he died and which she never wanted to wear. He shoved it far into his jeans pocket, then kept on searching. Ben was shocked to hear a banging on the apartment's front door. He heard Hao open it and several voices flooded the apartment. He searched the drawer desperately, one last time. At the last minute, his fingers curled around something familiar.

Got it!

He pulled out his mother's spare inhaler, feeling exhilarated. Holding on to it tightly, he dashed to the window and began to climb out. But all his hopes crumbled when the door crashed open. Hao rushed in, followed by another police officer.

Desperately, Ben threw the inhaler out the window just before they grabbed his arms. He shouted, "Fetch, Tike! Find Mom! Hurry!"

The two men pulled him back, Hao yelling down the corridor to another police officer, "Follow that dog!"

* * *

Down below, Tike bounced around wildly in circles. As soon as he saw a police officer appear from behind the building, he grabbed the inhaler between his teeth and darted back in the direction they had come.

The nimble Jack Russell ran as fast as his little legs would carry him. Even though he quickly lost the police officer, he charged on as if he was being pursued by hungry hounds. Being a smart dog, he did not have any trouble finding his way back to the Skytrain that he had taken with Ben over an hour ago. This took him back to the Waterfront Station where he zigzagged past commuters down to the pier of the Seabus. He slipped into the ferry that crossed the Burrard Inlet back to North Vancouver, then waited for the bus to Deep Cove to open its doors to let in passengers. When a little girl pointed out the dog to her mom, Tike scurried to the back of the bus where he lay down under a seat, shivering uncontrollably, his mouth painfully wrapped around the inhaler.

By the time Tike got off the bus at Deep Cove, he was no longer running. He stooped low with his head down. He only stopped once to drink thirstily from a dripping water fountain before heading slowly to the marina where he found the motorboat safely tied up to the pier. The dog hopped into the boat, then sat down on the driver's chair. He looked around expectantly. When no one showed up, he dropped the inhaler at his feet, his tongue lolling.

The faithful terrier waited patiently for his master to appear until exhaustion took over. Then he curled up on the seat, his legs carefully wrapped around the precious inhaler as he closed his tired eyes.

CHAPTER 16 *Black Carpenters*

On the first floor of the Vancouver Police Department, in a small, windowless room with one table and two chairs, Ben waited. Although his heart fluttered with worry, he found himself distracted by a movement at the edge of the table. A carpenter ant crawled along its metal surface before heading down a table leg. Ben watched as it made its way to the floor before scurrying on towards the door.

If only I were your size...

In his mind's eye, Ben became the insect that darted over the gigantic floor, reaching the slit under the door, the brightly lit corridor, the elevator, the way out...

The door whipped open, and Inspector

James Hao entered. With one colossal foot, he crushed the ant, making Ben jump as his vision of freedom went dark. The inspector sat down opposite Ben in his neatly pressed suit and perfectly trimmed hair. He dropped a file on the desk while scrutinizing Ben as he flipped through the pages. He picked out a couple of pictures which he slid across the table.

Ben stared at them, puzzled. One picture showed pieces of glass, while the other had an enlargement of a fingerprint.

"Seven weeks ago," Hao began, "We recovered all evidence from the crash site that took place near your grandfather's property. At first, we couldn't figure out what these pieces of glass were doing in the middle of the field. When we put the pieces together, however, we realized it was the lens of a telescope with the faint trace of a fingerprint on it." He pointed to the picture on the left. "The fingerprint turned out to be yours."

He studied the boy for a while before continuing. "We believe you were there, on the night of *The Cosmic Fall*. We believe you witnessed everything, yet you did not come forward with Ryan Archer, to provide your version of facts and, perhaps, invaluable information to national security."

Ben fidgeted in his chair, distracted by an ant that was tickling him on the leg. He was at a loss as to what to reply.

"This isn't a game, boy," Hao growled. "Our country, our very lives may be at stake. It's imperative we find out if the culprits behind *The Cosmic Fall* are a risk to our nation, to our planet! I don't know what game Ryan Archer was playing when he failed to mention your involvement. Were he alive today, he would have been arrested for interfering with an ongoing national investigation. So if he told you to keep silent, you had better think twice about that!"

A heavy silence followed. Ben cleared his throat. "The thing is, I can't remember anything. The doctor says I have amnesia..." he lied weakly.

Hao didn't look impressed. He took out another picture. Ben gasped as he saw the image of himself talking to Mesmo at his grandfather's funeral.

"I see your memory is already improving," Hao said bitterly.

Ben stared from the picture to the inspector, then back again, his face drained.

"I want to know who that is," Hao said. "And you're going to tell me."

Someone knocked loudly on the door.

Before Hao could respond, a bald man with an authoritative look stepped in.

Twisted eyes!

Ben turned white as a bedsheet and shrank into his chair in shock.

Connelly did not heed him as he turned to Hao, saying, "I need to talk to you outside."

"Not now," Hao replied impatiently.

"This is urgent. It can't wait."

Hao tapped a pen against the table impatiently, then got up, gazing down at Ben as he closed the button of his suit jacket. He gestured towards Bordock, presenting him to Ben. "This is Agent Theodore Connelly. He's been an invaluable asset on *The Cosmic Fall* case. While I step out, I suggest you work on recovering your memory, kid. You wouldn't want to get into more trouble than you already are in." Hao left the room, oblivious to the long, cold glare that Bordock threw at the boy.

The door closed, leaving Ben on his own again. His skin crawled, and his head exploded with questions.

What is Bordock doing here?

If he was frightened before, now Ben was terrified.

* * *

"What is it?" Hao hissed impatiently at Connelly, as they moved down the hall to avoid being overheard by the police officer placed in front of the room where Ben was being held.

"The Representative for the Children and Youth office is sending a lawyer to defend the kid," Connelly said in a low, urgent voice.

"A lawyer?" Hao exclaimed through gritted teeth. "I don't have time to deal with lawyers! How did they catch wind of this so quickly?"

"The office is automatically flagged when youth under the age of eighteen are arrested," Connelly explained.

"We can't have a lawyer poking around!" Hao said angrily. "We need to get a clearance from High Inspector George Tremblay and transfer the kid to the Dugout ASAP!"

Connelly insisted, "The local police are talking. They think we're drilling an underaged witness without giving him proper representation."

"The local police can say anything they want," Hao retorted. "This is a matter of national security! They have no idea what we're up against! No, the CSIS has precedence in this matter! I'll set all hounds loose on anyone who so much as approaches the boy." He pointed his index finger at Connelly. "I'll have Tremblay sign the transfer papers. That will allow us to override any questions from meddling lawyers or the RCMP. In the meantime, you keep an eye out. Make sure no one enters that room!"

"Wait!" Connelly cut in urgently as Hao walked away.

"What now?" Hao snapped.

"I have an idea that might convince Tremblay to speed things up."

Hao blinked at him. "What are you talking about?"

Connelly opened one side of his suit jacket, revealing a transparent vial that jutted out of his inside pocket. It contained a syringe and blood collection tube.

"We need to take a blood sample from the boy and have it analyzed," Connelly said.

Hao held up his hands to hide the contents of Connelly's pocket, glancing around to make sure no one had seen them. "Are you crazy?" he growled. "Not here, not now! There will be time for that later."

"No, hear me out!" Connelly urged. "I read in the files that the other witnesses had abnormal levels of lead in their blood after *The Cosmic Fall*. If the boy's blood matches that of the other witnesses, we'll have more undeniable proof that he was present. Besides, who knows what else we might find. Are we even sure he is who he says is?"

Hao shook his head. "You're jumping to a lot of conclusions. A blood sample at this stage is out of the question. If the boy talks to anyone..."

"He won't talk." Connelly interrupted in a convincing tone.

"That's beside the point," Hao continued. "If something like this were to get out we'd lose our jobs faster than you can blink."

"*I'd* lose my job," Connelly corrected. "I'll take the sample. If word should ever get out, I'll take the fall. I'm acting on my own. You're not aware of anything."

Hao stared at him, unconvinced.

Connelly insisted. "All I need is five minutes. Just think, if the blood reveals anything out of the ordinary, we'll be able to get all the clearances we need."

Hao looked around nervously. "All right," he said finally. "You have five minutes."

Connelly nodded, then turned away.

Hao called him back, "For the record, I don't

like your methods. They've proven effective so far, but you're on your own on this one. This conversation never took place."

Connelly nodded before heading to the interrogation room, while Hao took the elevator to the fifth floor where he began making phone calls from his makeshift office.

* * *

Ben ignored a second ant that crawled slowly across the table. Instead, he had his hand clamped feverishly onto his wristwatch, praying silently for Mesmo to appear. To his dismay, the door opened, and Bordock stepped in.

The boy and the bald man glared at each other. Fine sweat pearled Ben's forehead as he cowered deep in his chair, feeling like a trapped animal.

Without a word, Bordock shoved aside the second chair with his foot, then took out the transparent recipient, which he placed on the table. The ant scurried away. Carefully, Bordock opened the vial to take out the syringe and blood collection tube.

Ben's eyes widened. "What are you doing?" he asked fearfully.

Bordock removed the plastic wrapping from the syringe, answering, "Taking a blood sample."

Ben shook his head in protest, unable to speak.

Then, the alien pulled up the sleeve of his own, grey suit jacket and, still looking at Ben, pricked his own arm with the needle. Slowly, dark alien blood filled the syringe. Once he had filled it up, he pulled out the syringe, inserted the needle into the blood collection tube and transferred the thick liquid. He then stuck a small label onto the tube, writing on it with a black pen. BLOOD SAMPLE-BENJAMIN ARCHER.

"That's not my blood!" Ben croaked. "Why did you do that?"

Bordock finished wrapping everything up again. "To make sure they have a reason to keep you," he stated coldly.

"Why?" Ben whispered, barely able to speak from fear.

Bordock placed the recipient back in the inside pocket of his jacket. He squinted at Ben with his unnatural eyes, which changed from green to honey-brown. "For some reason," he said, "wherever I find you, I find Mesmo. So, as long as you are here, I am confident he will be joining us at some point." He straightened the front of his jacket, and added, "And if he doesn't, then the CSIS will find him for me."

Outside, in the corridor, they could hear Hao arguing loudly with a woman. Bordock's eyes narrowed threateningly. "You know what I'm capable of," he hissed. "I wouldn't say anything if I were you."

In that instant the door flew open, revealing a woman with blond, curly hair and modern, black glasses. She stared up and down at Connelly in a condescending way. "You! Out! I won't have anyone talking to my client."

Ben was glad she didn't notice the lethal look Bordock gave her as she placed a briefcase on the table. Addressing Ben in a business-like manner, she said, "You have the right to remain silent, Benjamin. You don't have to answer any of these men's questions. I'll be doing the talking for you from now on. My name is Barbara Jones. I've been assigned by the Representative for Children and Youth to represent you." As she clicked open the briefcase, she added, "In other words, I'm your lawyer."

She turned to face Connelly and Hao. The latter was seething at her from the corridor. "That will be all, gentlemen. You'll be hearing from my office when I'm done."

She closed the door on them. Both men walked away with quick strides.

"Did you get the blood sample?" Hao asked angrily.

"Yes," Connelly answered.

"Get it analyzed ASAP! We need to put a stop to this right away," Hao barked.

* * *

Barbara Jones sat down. "It's Benjamin Archer, right?"

Ben nodded, taken aback by this sudden shift of power.

She flipped through some documents in a very thin file, then pursed her lips, dissatisfied. "Well, they didn't leave me much to work with. I only have a home address and that you avoided questioning by law enforcement."

She closed the file before staring at Ben over the rim of her glasses.

"So," she began, showing interest in him for the first time. "Let's hear it."

Ben stared at her with his mouth open, "I... er... what do you mean?" He was excruciatingly aware of Bordock's proximity.

Barbara Jones moved forward in her chair,

accidentally crushing a carpenter ant with her arm as she leaned on the table. "Look, honey, my office had me move my schedule around just for you because you are a minor. I'm here to defend you, okay? That means that whatever you did, you can tell me. My job is to get you out of here as soon as possible."

She waved her hand at him, inviting him to speak. One large ant was climbing up the sleeve of her white shirt while another one was crawling across her closed file.

"So, let's have it," she repeated.

Ben was distracted by the ants.

How did so many get in here?

"I... " he began, his mouth dry as parchment.

Bordock could be listening right behind the door!

Ms. Jones became impatient. "Honey, I have thirty minutes to listen to your story before they kick me out of here. Let's see, how about we start with something easy, okay? For example, you can give me your dad's phone number. I promise I'll call him up as soon as I leave. How about that?"

Ben stared at her helplessly, "I... don't have a dad. He died in an accident after I was born."

The lawyer closed her eyes for a second, as an ant crawled up her cheek. She brushed it away with a motion of the hand as she arranged a strand of curly hair behind her ear.

"All right," she said a bit more gently. "How about your moth... Ouch!" she yelled, brushing at her arm. "Something bit me!" she gasped, her face flushed. She shrieked and bolted out of her chair, massaging her leg. She noticed the carpenter ants scurrying over the table, on her arms, on her legs, up her neck. She yelled again as they bit her. She brushed at them frantically, bobbing up and down like a ragged doll on a spring.

The police officer who had been standing guard in front of the room rushed in. "What's going on?" he demanded.

"Let me out of here!" she yelled, bouncing around. "Ouch!" She gestured towards Ben. "Get that boy out. This room's infested with ants... eek! Get him to a washroom! And call pest exterminators or something." She darted down the hall, distraught.

The policeman noticed the ants crawling all over Ben, and hurriedly led him down a couple of doors to the men's toilets. "Get in there and clean yourself up," he ordered, yelling as he was bitten in the neck.

Ben did as he was told, suddenly finding himself all alone in the washroom of the Police

Department.

As he stood there, gathering his senses, the carpenter ants that had been crawling all over him scurried to the floor, then vanished into the cracks in the wall. Ben checked his clothes, then stared in the mirror. All the ants were gone, leaving him without a single bite mark.

Jeepers!

Breathing fast, he turned his attention to the door which he locked in an automatic gesture. He leaned his head against it, closing his eyes dizzily. When he looked up again, Mesmo stood by the sinks, his face ashen. Ben let out a sob of relief.

"Ben," Mesmo said softly yet urgently. "I don't have much time! Turn on the taps."

Ben sniffed and nodded hurriedly. He opened all the taps to let water flow into the four sinks.

Mesmo indicated that the boy should move away from the door. The alien placed his hands in the stream of water, which immediately obeyed the energy that emanated from them. The liquid flowed horizontally against the wall then dripped to the floor. It spread out swiftly, covering the main door and doorknob before racing across the tiles. Ben had to move back until he was against the wall next to a toilet. Even there, the water

232

flowed along the wall up to a window located right above Ben's head. The whole washroom was covered in water that danced to a silent song, obeying the mysterious force that came forth from Mesmo like a magnet.

In an instant, the swirling motion stopped, then the water froze. The door became white, the doorknob crackled under the weight of the ice and the floor glistened with a slippery sheen.

Above him, Ben heard the bars in front of the window snap from the cold.

"Go on!" Mesmo encouraged him.

Ben clambered onto the closed toilet bowl, then shoved open the window. The metal bars which had snapped from the cold easily slid away before falling to the ground below. He pulled himself up, saw that he would be able to fit through and that the ground wasn't too far down. He turned to Mesmo, only to find him gone. "Mesmo!" he whispered.

Someone banged on the door, calling him to open up.

Ben wasn't going to wait around this time.

CHAPTER 17 *Granville*

Hao rushed past the frantic lawyer, saw the empty interrogation room, then joined the policeman who was trying to force open the door of the washroom.

"What's going on? Where's the boy?" he yelled angrily.

"He's in there. Locked himself up." The policeman grunted as he shoved his weight against the door.

Hao pushed him aside to grab the doorknob, then yelled as his hand burned from the freezing temperature of the metal.

"I don't care how you do it, you get this door open pronto!" he barked.

Another large policeman joined them. After

three attempts at throwing themselves with full force at the door, it gave, and they crashed in a heap inside.

Hao clambered over them, then fell heavily to the ground as he slipped on the sheet of thin ice that covered the floor. Groaning, he got back up. After several slippery attempts, he reached the open window.

"He's out!" Hao yelled as he peeked through the window into the street. "Go! Go! Go!" he ordered the policemen, who were slipping and sliding over the frozen floor.

* * *

Ben raced down the street. As he was about to turn a corner, he risked a glance back, only to find Hao and a couple of police officers barging out of the Vancouver Police Department after him. Turning the corner, he had to stop and lean against a wall. Dizziness had grasped his mind, and he swayed. Was he having a panic attack? He shut his eyes tight, forcing his breathing to slow.

Not now!

He ignored the stitch in his side and thudded on. As his lonely footsteps hit the pavement, Tike's absence weighed heavily on him. He crossed a busy road to the Skytrain station, then froze when a police car rounded a corner, placing itself at the very entrance. He backtracked hurriedly across the street. Hao appeared only a block away.

Ben slapped desperately on the door of a bus that was about to drive away. The driver frowned disapprovingly but let him in anyway. Ben hopped on, catching his breath as he saw Hao pointing in his direction. To his dismay, the bus headed southwest instead of north. His mind raced.

Granville Island!

If he could make it to the small peninsula that was a hotspot for tourists, he could get lost in the crowds and find another transport north. Ben glanced around fearfully. He spotted a police car with its lights whirling in the distance, as it zigzagged through traffic. It caught up with the bus a short distance from Granville Island. Ben hit the emergency button, and the doors swung open. Hao was getting out of the police car, when a throng of sports cyclists whizzed by, giving Ben the opportunity to dash down to the well-stocked public market. He pushed through groups of people strolling around the small, quaint streets strewn with art galleries, restaurants and artisan shops.

If only I could reach the marina!

He knew there was an Aquabus that could take him across to the City of Vancouver, with its skyscrapers, a short distance across the river. Too late, he glimpsed a police officer checking things out in the direction he was headed. Ben's heart raced as he felt his options of escape narrowing. He ducked into the large indoor market, making his way through the crowd of tourists who were picking out perfectly formed fruits and vegetables. The tourists gasped as Ben ran into them, making them accidentally knock over a pyramid of neatly arranged oranges which tumbled to the ground. Ben didn't have time to apologize. He dove out of the market and faced the other side of the marina, which was cluttered with pleasure boats and ferries.

Behind him, Hao pushed his way through the crowds inside the market.

Ben ran down a pier, bumping into people taking pictures of the scenery. At the end of it, tourists donned bright, orange fishermen waders and matching waterproof jackets with large hoods. Ben squeezed into this group. A stack of the orange garments lay on the floor, placed there for the tourists who were getting ready for a trip out to sea.

Without hesitating, Ben grabbed a large pair of pants and a jacket, putting them on in a hurry, copying what the other men and women were doing. Not a moment too soon, as a police officer, closely followed by Hao, appeared above the pier. They scanned the area with their eyes.

A tourist wearing the bright fisherman combination stood up, leaving a corner of a bench unoccupied, so Ben slipped onto the seat, trying to blend in with the crowd.

"It's almost time!" the woman next to Ben said excitedly.

He turned in surprise. An old woman with wrinkled cheeks and sunken eyes stared at him with a big, false-teeth smile.

"Is this your first trip, son?" she asked.

Ben checked his surroundings anxiously. Hao approached the entrance to the pier. Hastily, the boy turned to the old woman, who looked like she might be eighty, or closer to ninety. "Er... yes," he said vaguely.

"This is my forty-fifth trip!" she said proudly. "I met my late husband, Harold, on a trip like this, forty-five years ago! We would celebrate our wedding anniversary every year by making the same trip again." Her voice faltered only slightly, immediately replaced by her smile again. "You might think I'm a silly old lady, but I know Harold's spirit is watching over me today. I remember my first contact with the giants... oh, my! What a sight...!"

She chatted on. Ben no longer listened. Hao had jogged up behind the group of tourists and was asking them questions.

In the same instant, the orange-clad men and women trooped in front of a ferry which they began to board. Ben followed the flow with the old woman not far behind. A young, strong-built sailor who was asking for boarding tickets caught him by the arm. "Hey! Ticket, please!" he said with a strong accent.

Ben pointed to the people lining up behind him. "Uh... my Gran has them." He pushed on swiftly behind the other tourists, heading straight to the back of the ferry and several rows of outdoor benches. He hunched down as far away as possible from the ferry ramp, next to enthusiastic tourists who chatted in an array of different languages.

There was a bit of commotion on the ramp as the muscular sailor with a tight, black T-shirt requested tickets from the old lady.

"Oh, dear," she said worriedly. "Oh, where

did I put that ticket?"

An imposing man with broad shoulders and a captain's hat emerged from the bridge to inquire about the delay. When he noticed the old woman, he said with a thick, Australian accent, "Mrs. Stenner! Welcome aboard! I hadn't realized it was that time of the year already."

"Oh, Captain, I feel so foolish, I don't know where I put my ticket," she answered, dismayed.

"Two tickets." The stern-faced sailor corrected behind them. "She's also missing her grandson's ticket."

"Grandson?" the woman asked, confused.

The Captain waved a hand at the sailor, dismissing him, then, smiling, gently led the old lady to a front seat. "Come, I'm sure everything is fine. After all, you're our most faithful customer, aren't you, Mrs. Stenner? How many years has it been, exactly?"

"Forty-five!" the woman replied, returning his smile.

"Forty-five!" the Captain exclaimed, "Crikey! How about that! And you brought your grandson along this time? What a wonderful idea!"

Mrs. Stenner stared at him, at a loss for a few seconds, before her eyes brightened suddenly and she giggled, "Yes... er... of course! My grandson!

Lovely lad!"

"Good. Well, enjoy your trip, Mrs. Stenner. I must get up to the bridge as we are leaving in a couple of minutes," the Captain said, saluting her by lightly lifting his hat.

No sooner had the groups of families and friends of different nationalities settled on the benches, than the ferry moved away from the pier, heading out the harbour entrance into the open sea.

The Captain's voice boomed over the loudspeakers. "Ladies and gentlemen. This is Captain Oliver Andrew speaking. Welcome aboard the Haida Gwai II. The weather is looking fair as we head across the Strait of Georgia for our four-hour whale watching trip. We are happy to announce that several orca pods have been spotted in the past weeks. We should be in for quite a show..."

Four hours!

At the back of the ferry, hunched on the edge of a bench, Ben's face had gone pale as they moved away from Granville Island, away from the shore and further away from his mother.

At the edge of the pier, Hao paced up and down the marina, giving orders over the phone to spread out the search.

* * *

Susan Pickering sat by Laura's side as she finished taking her temperature. When she saw the number on the thermometer, she pursed her lips as she stared out the window. Laura's fever still had not broken. Being a nurse with experience, she knew that was not a good sign. She stroked the sick woman's arm, saying in a low voice, "Come on, Laura, you have to fight this!"

To her surprise, the young woman opened her eyes a crack. Through pale, dry lips she managed to ask, "Ben?"

Susan had to look away so that Laura wouldn't notice the worry on her face. Then she smiled reassuringly. "He's fine. He's resting—as should you."

Laura seemed satisfied with the answer because she closed her eyes again.

Susan stayed next to her for a long moment, staring out the window—biting her lip as she wondered what had happened to the boy.

* * *

The room was large and impeccably white.

Two men in green protective suits talked together quietly, analyzing the data on their computer screens behind a glass window, as Mesmo lay inside a full-body CT scan machine. He had been tranquillized and was unaware of what was going on.

Until now.

"He's waking up," one of the men said.

"Ok, let's pull him out," the other one replied after a while. "It's no use anyway."

He pressed a red button, releasing the motorized examination table which hummed slowly out of the machine.

A third man entered the room behind them. The two radiographers recognized him immediately in spite of his green protective suit and mouth cover. He was slightly shorter and heavier built than the other two.

"Boss," they said in a manner of greeting, straightening in their seats.

The man nodded briefly, before entering the examination room. He bent over Mesmo, who blinked as he tried to regain focus. The alien's eyes focused on the thick black and grey eyebrows overshadowing small, green eyes behind the man's black glasses.

"Well?" the third man asked with authority,

directing his question to the two radiographers.

"Still nothing, Sir," the younger of them answered. "Even after using the tranquillizer, we are getting the same interference."

"Show me!" the man ordered.

The two men sitting behind the window glanced at each other, uncertain. "Going through the procedure again could put a strain on his heart, Sir," the younger man ventured.

"Do it!" the boss insisted, joining them with determined strides.

Immediately the younger man obeyed. He pressed the red button again so that the examination table rolled slowly back into the tunnel-shaped machine.

Mesmo struggled against the straps holding his arms as he entered the claustrophobic hole of the CT scan.

CHAPTER 18 *Humpback*

As Susan Pickering's motorboat bobbed up and down in the bay of Deep Cove, Tike woke to the sound of two men laughing loudly as they trudged along the pier with buckets, fishing rods and a picnic box. The terrier lifted his head to watch them curiously.

The men chatted and laughed as they loaded their motorboat which lay further down the pier. One of them pointed to the other side of the inlet, in the general direction of the island that was the Pickering woman's home.

Tike pricked his ears, alert. He picked up the asthma inhaler between his teeth before jumping onto the pier. He slowed down until he saw that the men were busy placing their gear near the front of the motorboat, then hopped nimbly on board, scurrying under a bench at the back. He glanced out nervously. The men had not seen him.

Not long after, the motor rumbled to life. Then they were off, zipping away over the waters straight to the opposite side of the inlet.

Tike waited patiently before emerging from his hiding spot. He peeked out to watch the approaching piece of jutting land on which Susan lived. As soon as the boat was close enough to the island, Tike emerged from under the bench. He grasped the asthma pump tightly with his jaws, then leapt into the air before falling full force into the swirling, cold water.

The impact came as a shock. The dog almost lost his grip on the inhaler as he spun round under the water. He moved his paws frantically, trying to reach the surface again.

Tike's head emerged between the waves. He swam feverishly with his ears back and the white of his eyes showing. The small waves lapped at his face; the salt stung his eyes, the cold was numbing. No matter how hard he paddled, his short legs didn't seem to be bringing him any closer to the shore. Water entered his throat. His jaw hurt from holding the inhaler and exhaustion took over.

Soon only his snout stuck out from the water.

Tike stopped swimming, surrendering to the flow of the tides. The dog sank down into the water...

...and his paws touched sand.

In a last effort, the valiant canine began swimming again, pushing against the sand to move forward, until his head was completely out of the water. He reached smooth rocks which lay close to the surface. They allowed him to cover the last meters to the shore, where he stepped out onto the beach next to the short pier that he and Ben had left that very morning.

* * *

Inspector James Hao contacted his men as he paced the walkway in front of Granville Market. The reports were fruitless: the boy was nowhere to be found. He scanned the river and harbour opening as he spoke over the phone, excruciatingly aware of how many small sailing ships and motorboats were coming and going. It was going to take a lot of manpower to check every boat stationed within the small harbour, one by one.

He had barely hung up when his phone

rang. It was Connelly.

Hao filled him in on what had happened at the Police Department, including the ant incident, followed by the boy's escape from the frozen bathroom. When he finished, there was silence at the other end of the line.

"What is it?" Hao asked, fully expecting Connelly to accuse him of making the whole thing up.

Instead, Connelly replied slowly, "Well, that makes sense."

"What do you mean?" Hao asked.

"The preliminary results from the boy's blood test have arrived. They need further research, but the evidence is already pretty conclusive."

"Well?" Hao urged.

"The blood sample does not match that of the other witnesses," Connelly said. "Rather, it matches that of the aliens."

Hao put his hand through his black hair streaked with grey above the ears, pacing from one end of the walkway to the other, as Connelly's words slowly sank into his mind. "What are you saying?"

The agent's voice came clearly over the phone. "What I'm saying, is that the boy's blood is not human." He paused for effect, before adding, "It looks like we've found ourselves another alien."

* * *

On the island in the middle of the Burrard Inlet, Susan Pickering finished filling a basket with wood for the fire.

She walked back to her cabin, only to find the door ajar. She stepped inside carefully, noticing small, wet prints on the kitchen floor. The area around the dog's bowls was littered with crumbs of dog food and splashes of water. The paw prints went towards Laura's bedroom.

"Ben?" Susan called urgently.

She dropped the basket, then rushed to the back, pushing open the bedroom door. She found a very ruffled Tike rolled up in a ball on the bed, fast asleep.

Laura's head was propped up on a pillow with her eyes open. In one hand she was grasping an asthma inhaler. She showed it to Susan, saying with a frail voice, "Where's Ben?"

* * *

The Haida Gwaii II sped onwards across the Strait of Georgia, heading further and further away from Granville Island.

Ben lay hunched over his knees, his feet resting on the edge of the bench in front of him, his head down between his arms. Around him groups of people chatted away excitedly over the loud humming of the motors, making funny faces as they took each other's pictures in their fancy orange suits and life jackets.

Others were reading the whale watching company pamphlet, trying to memorize the names of the different types of whales they might encounter. The list was quite impressive, as it included Killer, Humpback, Minke and Blue whales, as well as Pacific white-sided dolphins.

Someone patted Ben on the back. He glanced up hurriedly.

"Have some chocolate," Mrs. Stenner, the old widow from the pier, said gently, offering him a chocolate bar. "You'll see, it will help with the seasickness." She waved the bar at him. He took it gratefully. "Harold's pockets were always full of them," she chatted amiably. "He didn't eat them himself, mind you. He was always careful about his diet, poor dear. No, he did it for me. He knew I would always ask him for one, my Harold did."

She stared into the distance, remembering.

Munching hungrily on the chocolate, Ben said with a full mouth, "I'm sorry I got you into trouble."

Mrs. Stenner clicked her tongue. "Tut, tut! I won't hear of it. My Harold always paid for two tickets, and so I shall, too, this year!" She patted him on the leg, before adding, "You relax, dear, enjoy the trip. You'll see, when you get back, everything will be all right." She got up, humming to herself as she strolled around the boat.

Ben sighed, then decided to explore the boat as well. It was made of three decks: the bridge deck with the cockpit, the main deck with outer and inner rows of benches to accommodate the tourists, and the lower deck with machinery and the captain's quarters. Thick, white clouds rolled across the sky, once in a while letting some sunshine through, while seagulls swooped around them, squawking. Ben wasn't invested in the scenery around him. The fact that he had had a panic attack on Susan's motorboat that morning crossed his mind, yet all he could think of was his mom and Tike. How was his dog ever going to make it all the way to Susan's island?

I miss you!

With a heavy heart, he settled down near the

front of the boat, below a jutting window from the indoor tourist area. Great exhaustion came over him. It had been a long day, full of intense emotions. The boat's engines ran smoothly, carrying the craft evenly over the water. The sound lulled him. The occasional sunshine warmed him as he huddled from the sea breeze. Before long his head bobbed until it rested against the wall, and he fell into a deep sleep.

* * *

About two and a half hours later, up in the cockpit of the Haida Gwaii II, Captain Oliver Andrew was sipping on a cup of hot coffee, when a crewman turned and stretched out the speaker from the marine VHF radio to him, "Captain, it's the Coast Guard. They want to speak to you directly."

The broad-faced Captain picked up the receiver, speaking with a distinctly Australian accent. "Captain Andrew here, over." He listened for several minutes, before saying, "That seems highly unlikely, Sir. But send over the report: I'll have it checked out by my crew. Over and out."

He hung up, drummed his fingers on the dashboard impatiently, then turned as the fax machine came to life. A crewman picked up the printed document and handed it to him. The Captain read it with curiosity.

"J-Pod, three miles northwest," a crewman announced, pulling the Captain out of his thoughts.

Captain Andrew placed the arrest warrant with Ben Archer's face on it on the table, then took his binoculars to inspect the area of interest.

A family of about twenty orca—also called an orca pod—frolicked in the open waters some distance ahead.

"That oughta keep Mrs. Stenner happy," the Captain muttered half to himself, though the crewman overheard him and chuckled.

Behind them, the young sailor who had been checking the boarding tickets entered. He searched his jacket hanging from a hook in the wall, pulled out a sandwich wrapped in aluminum foil and sat down at the small table in the middle of the cockpit. He was about to take a big bite when the Captain noticed him. "Better hurry with that, Egor. I'm announcing a J-Pod in two minutes."

The tanned sailor with tattoos on his muscled arms pulled the sandwich away from his mouth. "Yes, Captain." As he lifted the sandwich again, he spotted the upside-down arrest warrant. He gasped. "That's that old widow's grandson!" He said as he picked up the paper, turning it the right way up.

Captain Andrew let go of his binoculars in a hurry. "What did you say?"

Egor was still holding his sandwich in one hand and the paper in the other. He nodded towards Ben's face. "Yes, that's him, the boy who's travelling with that woman... What's her name again?" He frowned as he tried to remember.

"Mrs. Stenner?" the Captain offered.

"Yes, that's it! She couldn't find the boarding tickets for her grandson and herself, remember?"

The Captain and the sailor exchanged a glance as they began to grasp the situation.

"Get Mrs. Stenner up here, would you?" the Australian ordered.

"Yes, Captain!" Egor answered, rising quickly, the sandwich now forgotten on the table.

The engines stopped close to the orca pod as the young man left the table in search of Mrs. Stenner. Over the loudspeaker, the Captain invited the tourists to watch the black and white animals from the rear end of the deck, which they did in an instant, clicking their cameras as the animals played in the water.

In the cockpit, Captain Andrew could hear Mrs. Stenner's voice long before she reached the top of the stairs. As soon as Egor opened the door for her, she exclaimed excitedly. "Thank you so much for inviting me up here, Captain! I..."

"Mrs. Stenner!" the Captain interrupted, holding up his hand to silence her. "Please, Mrs. Stenner, didn't you say you were travelling with your grandson? I was hoping you might have brought him up here with you."

The old widow stared at him blankly. "Grandson? What grandson?"

Captain Andrew scowled as he waved the arrest warrant in her face. "This grandson?"

She squinted to see the image better, then giggled. "Oh! That boy! This is his first trip, you know? But that's not my grandson, by the way. I have six granddaughters and only one grandson! Can you imagine? He just turned three..."

"Mrs. Stenner!" Captain Andrew scolded. "Are you telling me you lied to me? And that I have a stowaway kid on board my ship?"

"Ooh!" Mrs. Stenner quipped, wide-eyed. "A stowaway! Well, how about that..." She stopped as Captain Andrew held up his hand again. He stared down at his feet with gritted teeth, fighting to remain calm.

"Blimey," he swore under his breath.

* * *

Ben woke up to excited shouting. He blinked and searched the boat with his eyes, then realized the tourists had flocked to the back of the ship to observe the group of orca that was apparently putting on quite a show. The ship's Captain spoke over the loudspeakers, explaining the nature of the orca family, where they came from, how old they were, what they ate, and even named some of the individuals, recognizing them by the shape of their tails and dorsal fins.

Ben didn't have the energy to participate in the excitement. He was still tired and hoped to catch some more sleep. At least that way he wouldn't have to listen to his worried thoughts or his grumbling stomach. He closed his eyes again but could not find any peace this time. He had an eerie feeling of being watched. When he realized there was no one else there, he settled down again.

That's when he saw a great humpback whale basking at the surface of the water right in front of him. Ben blinked, thinking at first it might be a large rock. Then he saw the big, black eye staring at him silently, as the beast swam along, accompanying the soft swaying of the boat.

Ben glanced around, discovering he was the only one who had noticed the huge mammal. He slid from his comfortable spot and approached the edge carefully, afraid any sudden movement might frighten the great beast away. It remained there, motionless, captivating him with its one huge eye. Boy and whale gazed at each other with curiosity. Ben felt an awe towards the animal that he had never before thought possible. In his mind, he could hear the muffled silence of the deep sea, while the immensity of the ocean reflected in the whale's eye. There was a sense of great freedom in the vastness of the open waters, away from the sounds of humming motorboats, of wind and rain, drifting at will for miles and miles.

"What are you looking at?" Ben said softly, as the whale swam level with him. "Are you going to keep me out of trouble?" he asked.

As if in answer, the whale spewed out a loud stream of air and water through its blow hole before sinking slowly beneath the surface like a ghost.

Beware...

"Hey, kid!" someone barked behind Ben. "Free ride's over now."

Ben whirled to face the sailor in his black t-shirt and jeans, suddenly feeling overwhelmingly nauseous, though he couldn't tell if it was from motion sickness from the boat or something brought on by the whale.

"You'd better come with me," the sailor said. "The Captain wants to speak to you."

He was standing very close to Ben to show he meant business. It crossed Ben's mind to make a run for it, but he had to give in to the obvious: there was nowhere to run to.

CHAPTER 19 *Haida Gwaii II*

When Ben entered the cockpit, closely followed by Egor, the Captain was waiting for him with his hands on his hips. The Australian was about to say something to the young sailor, when he wrinkled his nose. "Ugh, what's that smell?"

Egor fidgeted as he remained by the door. "Sorry, Captain. The kid threw up on my shoes on the deck."

The Captain glowered. "Well, what are you waiting for? Get cleaned up! And take care of that deck, too. I don't want anyone slipping and hurting themselves."

The sailor opened his mouth to object, but the Australian glared at him in warning. Egor straightened. "Yes, Sir!" he said hastily, exiting the cockpit.

Ben concentrated on remaining standing; his legs were like jelly. He felt terribly awkward standing before the Captain with his huge orange waders and jacket. The Captain waved him to the table so he could sit. The smell from Egor's abandoned roast beef sandwich left Ben's stomach churning, though, curiously, he couldn't tell whether it was from seasickness or extreme hunger.

"I'm Oliver Andrew, Captain of the Haida Gwaii II," the Australian introduced himself.

Ben glanced at him shyly. "I'm sorry I threw up on the deck," he said apologetically. "...and that I didn't pay for my ticket."

The Captain crossed his arms. "Do you think this is about an unpaid ticket, son?" he asked. "Tell me, do you know how many people are on board this ship?"

When Ben shrugged, the Captain explained, "There are forty-seven tourists and six crewmembers, me included. That's fifty-three in total. Fifty-three! Not one more, not one less. And I'm responsible for all of them. In case you hadn't noticed, we're way out in the middle of the Strait.

Should we run into any trouble, we'd be on our own here."

He paused to make sure he had the boy's attention. "So," he continued, "If we were to have problems, I'd be looking to save fifty-three people. Not fifty-four. If you were to slip and fall into the water, no one would know to look for you, because no one would have known you had snuck onto the boat." He turned to look out at the vast sea—Ben's eyes following his. "Do you see why you did a very irresponsible and dangerous thing?"

Ben stared at the floor.

I understand full well.

"Now," the Captain said. "For the safety of my passengers and crew, I want to know what's going on. Why are you here and what did you do, son?" He waved a finger at him.

Ben glanced up at him angrily. "I didn't do anything!"

Captain Andrew shoved the arrest warrant towards him. "That's not what it says here, mate. This CSIS guy seems to think otherwise."

Ben sat back, his heart sinking.

The Captain waited for him to respond. Since Ben didn't reply, he said, "Fine, have it your way." He took the paper from the table, then picked up the speaker from the marine VHF radio. "I'm sorry, son, whatever trouble you're in, you'll have to face the consequences. You're too young to be dragging arrest warrants behind you."

He said into the speaker. "Charlie Bravo One, Charlie Bravo One. This is Alpha Foxtrot. Come in. Over."

"Alpha Foxtrot. This is Charlie Bravo One. You are speaking to the Coast Guard. Go ahead. Over," a woman answered.

The Captain kept his eyes on Ben the whole time. "This is Captain Andrew Oliver from the Haida Gwaii II. Patch me through to Inspector James Hao from the CSIS. Tell him I have his suspect in custody. Over."

"Copy. Over."

There was a long silence, then a man's voice answered, "This is Inspector James Hao. Who is this? Over."

Ben's face paled as the Captain presented himself and explained the situation.

"Excellent work, Captain," Hao said. "Give me your location. I will dispatch an amphibious helicopter to pick up the suspect. Over."

The Captain stared at the receiver, somewhat taken aback, before replying, "Negative, Inspector. I will not have any disruptions to my trip, nor will I cause panic among my passengers with unusual maneuvers. We will head back to port immediately. We will arrive in less than an hour. Over."

The Captain listened expectantly. Then the radio crackled back to life.

Hao said, "Understood. You are not to let the boy out of your sight. He already escaped from the Vancouver Police Department this morning. Over."

The Captain glanced at Ben in surprise, then said, "I need to know what I'm up against. The arrest warrant is vague. Please elaborate. Over."

There was another silence before Hao replied icily, "This is a confidential matter relating to national security, Captain. I am not authorized to elaborate. We expect you here in one hour. Over and out."

The Captain bit his lip, unhappy with the answer, but said, "Roger that. Over and out."

He put down the speaker, inspecting Ben, who looked like he was about to throw up again. The Captain headed to the back of the cockpit, where he opened a cooler and fished out a Coke. He handed it to Ben, who gulped it down thirstily.

"Blimey!" Captain Andrew said. "Slow down, mate! The Coke will settle your stomach but don't overdo it!"

Ben put down the can, and eyed the sandwich hungrily. The Captain noticed. "Go on, eat it, if you think your stomach can handle it. You'll need a clear head when we arrive."

Ben didn't wait to be told twice: he chomped down on the sandwich as if he hadn't eaten in days. In the meantime, Captain Andrew gave orders to turn the boat around and head back to Granville Island. Ben was swallowing the last piece of bread when Egor returned. The sailor's eyes immediately fell on the empty aluminum foil. He glowered at Ben without saying anything.

Captain Andrew turned his attention to Ben again. "Shouldn't you be calling someone? Your mom? Your dad? To let them know you're safe?"

Ben bit his lip, then shook his head.

"There has to be someone," the Captain insisted.

"There is," Ben replied with great effort. "My mom. But she's very sick." He gazed pleadingly at the Captain, before blurting, "I don't want her to die! That's why I went to get her inhaler! I thought if I could treat her asthma, maybe she would get better..."

The Captain frowned as he lifted his hat to scratch his forehead. He sighed. "Listen, son, talk openly to that inspector. Explain things to him. I'm sure he will be reasonable."

Ben sank his head into his hands, mumbling, "I don't think so."

When he didn't elaborate, the Captain said, "Egor, take him down to my quarters." He turned to Ben again. "Go on, son, and don't try anything funny. I want to bring everyone back safe and sound. All fifty-four of us. Is that clear?"

Ben nodded, resigned. He followed Egor who had opened another door that led to stairs to the lower deck.

* * *

"What happened?" the man asked with a deep voice, as he drummed his fingers on the long, polished table, his thick golden ring shining. He stared out the window at the Toronto skyline without really seeing it.

Another man's voice answered over the phone. "It's just like we thought: it was his heart. The CT scan machine proved too much for him. We almost lost him."

The man adjusted his black-rimmed glasses while he sat in the elegant meeting room in a high-backed chair. His thick black and grey brows pulled together in a frown. "Is he awake yet?"

The voice at the other end said, "Not yet. Might be a while."

"I don't have a while!" the gold-ringed man said impatiently. "I need answers! And I need them soon!"

The other man said calmly, "If we keep on pushing, you may never get any answers at all."

The man in the meeting room drummed his fingers even harder, mulling things through.

His contact continued, "We have an idea as to why we 'lose' him so often. We think he uses a mechanism that puts him in survival mode, like bears when they go into hibernation. He's capable of shutting down organs. He crawls into a shell to save energy. What happened in the CT scan, however, was different. He went into shock this time. He must not have been expecting it. He panicked and didn't have time to go into that hibernating state."

The man in the meeting room stood up and walked over to the window. In an agitated voice, he exclaimed, "I don't care what shell he crawls into. You find a way to prod that alien out! I was supposed to have results. Now everything is delayed!" He paced before the window, staring down twenty-four floors to the street below. "My flight leaves tomorrow. I'll be gone for three months to oversee the site. Let's hope our business partners don't lose patience. Our Martian fellow had better be ready to talk by the time I get back."

The man at the other end of the line said, "I'll make sure that he is."

* * *

Ben tried the doorknob several times, though he already knew it was locked. He turned to scan the Captain's quarters. On the left was a closet, and near the windows was a small sofa attached to the wall. On the right, he noticed a desk with a neat pile of documents, a sextant, and a picture of the Captain with his arm around a smiling woman and two children: a boy about Ben's age, and a smaller girl. Ben stared at the picture for a while.

They seem so happy.

On his way to look out the window, Ben struggled to move. The waders and jacket were cumbersome in this cramped room, so he removed his life jacket and both orange attires, then left them on the floor. He kneeled on the sofa, pulled the one side of the window that could slide open, and stuck out his head. A cold wind and ocean spray hit his face, making him squint. His hair blew in all directions.

He could make out the entrance of the sea arm that led to Granville Island in the distance, yet, what caught his attention, was that they were travelling past the red and white lighthouse where, some nights back, Laura and he had seen Mesmo disappear before their eyes.

Ben automatically reached for his watch. He rubbed it, wondering if Mesmo might come, but nothing happened. Ben glanced out the window again.

Should I jump?

The boat was moving fast, the waves lapping at the sides, while the lighthouse was quite a distance away. Even with a life jacket on, he wasn't sure he could make it. The Captain's words rang in his mind, "If you were to slip and fall into the water, no one would know to look for you."

Ben pulled back, closed the window, and gazed around helplessly.

* * *

Inspector James Hao was joined by Agent Theodore Connelly and a police officer on the pier where the Haida Gwaii II had docked moments ago. The tourists were asked to descend one at a time. They threw curious glances at the officers as they headed back to the tourist stand of the company that had sent them on the whale watching trip.

Captain Oliver Andrew stood by, thanking the passengers as they left, while Mrs. Stenner approached him to say goodbye. "A memorable trip, as usual, Captain!" she gushed. "Though for the life of me, I could not find that boy again. He seems to have vanished into thin air!"

The Captain smiled gently. "Don't worry, Mrs. Stenner, we found him. He's in good hands."

"Oh, well then, I'm sure he is!" the old woman replied. "Don't be too hard on him, poor lad. Why, at his age, I would be skipping school to go swimming at the lake all day! Those are the memories that last. This boy is no different. He needs adventure and freedom. Don't squash that spirit in him!"

The Captain took her hands in both of his. "You are a wise woman, Mrs. Stenner. And you are right, as always." He winked at her.

"Goodbye, then, see you next year!" she smiled, waving at him.

She was one of the last passengers to disembark. She cast a vexed expression as Hao and Connelly pushed by without waiting for her to step onto the pier.

Hao presented himself and Connelly to the Captain, as they shook hands. The Captain invited them to follow him to the lower deck. On their heels was another police officer and Egor, the young sailor. When they stood before the Captain's quarters, Egor took out a key, turned it in the lock, and pushed the door.

It wouldn't budge.

Hao and Connelly exchanged a quick look before pushing Egor aside. They tried to shove open the door, only managing to do so with some effort. The Captain's desk blocked the way. They had to work to push it aside to gain access. As soon as Hao and Connelly were inside, they noticed the open window.

Connelly inspected the marina, with its many small boats and sail ships. "There!" he exclaimed. Hao followed his index finger as he pointed out to sea.

In the distance, they could make out a spot of orange from Ben's waders and life jacket drifting on the water, close to a pier on the opposite side of the small harbor.

Hao turned to face the Captain angrily. "I told you to keep an eye on him at all times! Weren't you listening when I told you he escaped once already?"

Captain Andrew looked embarrassed as he stuttered, "I... er... I didn't expect..."

Hao ignored him, turning to Connelly instead. "Let's go! Hurry, before the kid reaches the other side!"

Hao shoved past Captain Andrew and Egor, though not before saying menacingly, "This won't go without consequences, Captain!"

Captain Andrew shrugged helplessly, then watched as the inspector, the agent and the police officer rushed away.

* * *

All kinds of small sea vessels dotted the piers of Granville Island, some old and rusted, others gleaming and slick. It was a maze of pleasure boats. Hao and Connelly had a hard time finding their way to the correct pier from which they could fish Ben out of the water.

After a couple of wrong turns, they made it to the end of a pier from which they spotted the orange waterproof jacket floating on the lapping waves.

The police officer who was accompanying them clambered down a short ladder to the water level. He reached out to catch Ben as he drifted past, but all he found was an empty, rolled up jacket which bulged with a pocket of air.

The three men glanced in surprise at the piece of clothing. They searched all around for the missing boy who was supposed to be wearing it. He was nowhere to be found.

Connelly swore. "He tricked us!"

Hao exclaimed, "The ship! He never left the ship!"

CHAPTER 20 *Paddleboard*

Laura sat carefully on the edge of the bed, her feet dangling a few inches above the wooden floor, as she drank a creamy soup that Susan had served her. The hot liquid that slid down her throat felt terrific. For the first time in many days, her strength was returning.

She patted Tike on the head, praising him. "Good dog!"

Tike's tongue lolled happily.

"Where's Ben, Tike?" she asked softly. The Terrier jumped off the bed, then rushed out into the kitchen with his tail wagging.

Laura tried to get to her feet to follow him when Susan entered. "Whoa, girl! Back into bed with you. This is no time to go for a jog."

She ushered Ben's mother back under the bedsheets. Laura opened her mouth to object, but her face had already drained of energy. Although she was no longer hungry, she accepted some toast with cream cheese and forced herself to continue eating, determined to get well as soon as possible.

Tike peeked back into the room to check whether Laura was following him. When he saw that she had gone back to bed, he trotted out of the house, over the grass, then down to the short pier. Once he had reached the end of it, he sat down, staring out over the water, waiting for his master to return.

* * *

In the Captain's quarters in the hull of the Haida Gwaii II, a soft breeze entered through the open window. Below it, a couple of seals rolled playfully in the water. A door squeaked open, and Ben stepped out of the Captain's closet. He had to push the desk, as it was blocking his way. Soon he stood in the middle of the room, listening for sounds.

When satisfied he was alone, he carefully stepped into the corridor, up the stairs and into the cockpit. Since there was no one there, he gathered courage, opened the door leading out, and hurried down the exterior stairs, at the end of which he could see the ramp connecting the ship to shore.

As Ben hopped down the last step, Captain Andrew appeared from the back of the ship, which had been out of Ben's range of vision.

The boy froze. He watched the Australian, who only had to take one large stride to block Ben's access off the ship.

"Smart bloke, aren't you?" the Captain said, observing him with his arms crossed. "That's what I'd figured."

Ben found his voice. "What are you going to do?"

Captain Andrew sighed, "I don't know. I guess that depends on you."

Ben swallowed hard. "What do you mean?"

Egor came running up behind the Captain. He spotted Ben and wanted to grab him. The Captain held up his arm, indicating he should stand back. Egor stared at his boss in surprise.

"I have a son, you see," the Captain said, concentrating on Ben. "He's about your age. And if he were in trouble, I'd want to be sure he came to his mother or me for help."

"I told you," Ben said desperately. "That's exactly what I'm trying to do. I'm trying to reach my mother!"

Egor turned away from them, then said hurriedly, "Captain, those policemen are heading this way again."

Ben was stricken as he stared at the Captain.

Slowly, the Captain stepped back. With a movement of his head, he said, "Go on then. I choose to believe you. Go help your mom."

Ben rushed forward, but the Captain stopped him again. "Wait," he said, as he handed him a life jacket. "Take this and wear it. I don't want to be fishing you from the bottom of the harbour."

Ben took it. "Thank you," he said earnestly. The Captain got out of the way so that Ben could escape down the ramp.

"Don't make me regret this!" was the last thing he heard the Captain shout behind him.

* * *

Tike sat at the end of the pier, observing the inlet and the mountains. Suddenly he stood, his body weight rolled forward, his tail lifted and his ears pricked. He remained like that, listening attentively. On the surface, the lapping waves and a soft breeze blowing through the fir trees could be heard.

Only the most trained ear or high-end underwater hydrophones would have been able to capture the sound that was travelling deep below the surface of the inlet. The ethereal vocalizations of the humpback whale went from low to high-pitched clicks, echoing far and wide until they reached Tike's ears.

The dog froze, fully alert, one paw lifted from the ground, until he could take it no longer. He darted up and down the pier in excitement.

Realizing there was nothing he could do to respond, Tike sprinted back to the cottage like a bouncing ball.

* * *

Ben ran away from the Haida Gwaii II. The only way off the pier was blocked by the approaching police officers. He had no choice but to find another way to escape.

He bent over, hiding between two ships, when a movement in the water caught his eye. He glanced down, noticing another, lower pier, almost at water level. Beside it, two seals swam playfully. But it wasn't the seals that had caught his attention. Instead, on the edge of this pier, lay a lime green paddleboard and black paddle, ready for use.

Ben looked around, wondering who it might belong to. There was no one else in sight. He bit his lip, trying to decide what to do, as he did not like the idea of stealing. What convinced him, however, was the image of the lighthouse he had seen from the Haida Gwaii II when they first motored into the Burrard Inlet. The idea of boarding to a safe place won out over his fears. Relieved at having some sort of plan to distance himself from the searching men, Ben hurriedly put on the life jacket, placed the paddleboard in the water, and began paddling between the boats until he was close to the harbour exit. Full of determination, he left the harbour, Granville Island, the Inspector, and Bordock behind.

* * *

Tike scurried into Laura's bedroom excitedly.

She sat in a chair by the window, looking out to the bay and biting her fingernail. "What is it, Tike?" she asked.

The terrier sprinted to the door, running back-and-forth to catch her attention.

Laura did not doubt the dog's intelligence. She found her slacks, shirt, and sweater, and followed Tike out of the house. She was halfway across the lawn when Susan called out, "Laura! What are you doing? You're in no shape to be wandering around like that!"

Laura said with full determination, "Ben needs me. I can't wait any longer. I'm going to find my son and I won't let you stop me!"

There were dark patches under her eyes, and she swayed slightly. Susan held on to her arm.

"All right!" the woman answered reluctantly. "All right! We'll both go. But we have to be smart." She frowned, thinking hard. "You go on to the boat," she decided. "I'll get jackets, your inhaler, the car keys, and some other things. Do you think you can make it?"

Laura nodded, though she seemed terribly frail.

The two women split ways. Laura cautiously made her way to Susan's second motorboat, following Tike, who was already waiting for her at the pier.

Before long, both women and the dog were speeding across the inlet towards Deep Cove.

* * *

Sailboats dotted the bay, their owners enjoying what was probably going to be one of the last mild days before the coming winter. Further out, huge container ships were anchored, waiting for their turn to unload their cargo at the Vancouver Harbour. Behind them were the shores of North Vancouver bordered by the North Shore Mountains. Following this coastline westward with his eyes, Ben spotted the lighthouse he was heading for.

Jeepers! It's miles away!

Somehow, looking out from the hull of the Haida Gwaii II a couple of hours ago, the distance from the lighthouse to Granville Island had seemed very short. Of course, he had been on a sturdy, fast-moving boat. Now, he was a tiny speck on the bay with the City of Vancouver and Stanley Park slowly moving away from him as he paddled furiously.

He had been so eager to get away from Granville Island! He wasn't ready to admit yet that trying to reach the lighthouse was a big mistake.

I won't make it...

CHAPTER 21 *The Breach*

Once they had docked the motorboat and recovered Susan's car from the shed, both women and Tike drove off towards Deep Cove. Laura assumed Ben would have headed to their apartment. She clung to the faint hope that he might still be there. She wouldn't hear of Susan contradicting her, even though she knew it was a dangerous decision to go there.

Susan headed to the bridge that would take them into Burnaby, driving well over the speed limit. Suddenly, Tike went crazy in the back seat. He jumped frantically onto Laura's lap, almost causing Susan to crash.

Susan yelled in surprise. "What's wrong with that dog? Make him stop!"

Laura replied quickly, "No! We should pay attention to him. I think he knows where Ben is. He'll take us to him." She held the terrier gently, urging him, "Go on, Tike, find Ben. Find him!"

Tike pricked his ears. He gazed determinedly out the window to Laura's right.

"Turn back! We need to head further west," she ordered Susan.

"But..." Susan began.

"Susan! Please!" Laura begged.

Susan stared at Laura and shook her head in disapproval but did as she was told.

* * *

Ben was only halfway across the bay by the time the sun had descended on the horizon. When he realized he was almost at a standstill, he sat on the board, his head dropping, his legs dangling in the cold water. His arms were numb with the effort of constant paddling. He shut his eyes tight, shivering under the weight of the infinite firmament above and the cold water below. A small plane flew overhead. Ben forced himself to wave at it—even though he knew it was futile; there was no way they would notice him from up there.

Mesmo! Where are you?

He wished the alien would magically appear to save him again, but Mesmo's words echoed in his mind. "If you cross this inlet, I can't guarantee that I will be there to help you."

Ben lay down on the paddleboard, exhausted. His dog's absence from his side weighed heavily on his heart.

Mom! Tike!

Something thumped at the back of the paddleboard. Ben gasped in fear and pulled up his legs as he turned to see what had hit him.

The head of a brown seal popped out of the water, observed him curiously, then disappeared again under the board. Before him, another seal appeared. Ben watched as both animals flipped and pirouetted at great speed.

"You're the ones from the harbour!" he exclaimed.

He relaxed, realizing that they were not out to harm him. Instead, the big, black eyes of the good-natured mammals invited him to join them in their underwater game.

Play! They seemed to say.

Their whiskers glistened with droplets as they waited for him to react. All Ben could do was shiver with cold.

"Help me!" he begged through shivering lips.

Immediately, one of the seals grabbed onto a rope that was tied to the front of the board, tugging at it briefly. The rope disappeared into the water, as did the seals, but a moment later, Ben felt another tug. The paddleboard moved forward slightly, and suddenly Ben found himself being pulled across the bay.

Ben was dumbfounded at his luck, though he had to lie down as he began to feel dizzy. Drops of water sprayed into his face. He closed his eyes. He tried to stay awake, but the constant up-and-down movement of the board lulled him.

The seals surfaced, then dove again in a kind of dance-like movement. Ben didn't know whether he was awake or dreaming. He felt as though he was dancing with them below the surface, twirling gracefully in a weightless world. He forgot about the heavy burden of the sky. He felt liberated. Nothing could touch him. His mind was free to wander and whirl below the waves. His heart leapt with excitement as he tried to keep up with his playful companions.

Then, suddenly, the marine mammals disappeared into the depths with one swift movement.

"Play!" Ben heard himself plead, longing for

the seals to keep him company. He blinked awake at hearing his own voice and found himself floating under the shadow of the mountains, not far from shore. He could make out small beaches separated by big, grey boulders topped with fir trees and, a short distance to the left, the towering lighthouse. The seals were gone.

Ben tried to stand on the paddleboard. His brain was strangely lightheaded as if he were suffering from seasickness again. How long he had been unconscious, he couldn't tell. The sky had become a soft pink reflecting on the calm waters. Gentle wisps of clouds were turning a brighter red while the mountains threw black shadows into the water.

So close!

He was only about ten yards from shore. He knew he had to put his mind and effort into reaching land, even though he ached as if he had been swimming for hours. His soaking wet clothes stuck to his body under the life jacket and he trembled uncontrollably.

After trying unsuccessfully to put some weight into his paddling, he glanced up at the imposing rock formation from which his mother had almost slipped and fallen some nights before. It seemed to taunt him to come closer.

That's when Ben spotted Mesmo.

The alien man was standing tall and proud on the ledge, roughly at the same place where Ben and his mother had found him on the night of the downpour.

The silhouette of a woman came running up beside him, followed by a small dog.

Ben's heart leapt into his throat. "Mom!" he yelled, exhilarated.

She saw him, waved, and yelled back, "Ben!"

Tike ran back and forth before her.

Ben's energy returned in an instant. He paddled as fast as he could.

Susan joined the others on the ledge. She and Laura searched for a way down to the small beach where Mesmo had helped Ben recover his memory. Laura headed down when she realized Mesmo had not budged. She followed his gaze out to sea—not towards Ben—but further away into the horizon.

Ben saw Mesmo raise his arm to point into the distance. He turned to see what had caught the alien's attention. He noticed the dot of a ship far away.

"Ben!" he heard his mother yell again, only this time the tone of her voice had changed. She was desperate.

He saw her point in the same direction as Mesmo. "Hurry!" she shouted.

When Ben looked behind him again, he was startled to see how quickly the ship had turned from a dot on the horizon to a fast approaching speedboat heading straight towards him. Ben's heart leapt into his throat.

I know who's on that boat!

He wanted to get to shore and safety, but his hands were frozen. He lost his grasp on the paddle in panic. It slipped into the water and began to drift away. Ben dropped to his stomach, frantically trying to reach for it. He could hear the motorboat roaring towards him. He spotted Mesmo, Laura, Susan, and Tike disappearing into the trees as they began clambering down the hill to reach the beach. Ben gave up on the paddle, resorting to his hands to move forward in the water, like a surfer.

It was useless.

In no time, the large motorboat passed him by, cutting off his path to the beach. Ben hung onto the paddleboard for dear life as the waves almost toppled him into the water. The motorboat went quiet after it maneuvered as close as possible to Ben. The boy's fingers curled tightly around the paddleboard even after the surface of the water had gone still. The dark blue metal of the ship pinged with static while the paddleboard thumped against its side.

After a moment, a rope ladder bounced down.

Hao called out, "Benjamin Archer!"

The boy lifted his head. The inspector stared down at him grimly. Next to him stood Bordock. Ben spotted a couple of police officers. The white letters on the side of the boat confirmed that it belonged to the Vancouver Police.

"Climb aboard!" Hao ordered.

Ben searched around with his eyes: his mother and Mesmo were nowhere to be seen. Overwhelmed with despair, he stood slowly on the paddleboard and stared helplessly at the rope ladder.

"We could wait here all night." Hao said impatiently. "You wouldn't last long. The temperature is dropping fast. So make a wise choice and get up here!"

Ben bit his blue, shivering lips. He knew the inspector was right.

I'll freeze if I stay out here much longer!

With a sinking heart, Ben grabbed onto the ladder, and put a foot on the first step.

Don't!

He stopped. Something in his mind was urging him not to take another step upwards. He glanced down at the space between the paddleboard and motorboat. It was very dark. Eerily dark. He stared at the water, transfixed.

Hao's voice was icy cold. "Benjamin Archer! Hiding is useless; I already know what you are."

What's he talking about?

Ben cast a look at Hao, then at Bordock, gritting his teeth. For a split second their eyes locked in a silent battle. Ben took his foot off the ladder and pushed himself away from the boat as hard as he could. Not that it mattered, as he only floated a couple of inches away. Hao lifted his arms in frustration.

Ben bent down on his knees, and slowly paddled away from the boat with his hands.

Hao shouted, "What do you think you're doing? Get back h..." He broke off in mid-sentence, his mouth wide open.

The massive humpback whale breached the surface. It soared like a huge mountain between the paddleboard and the motorboat as if in slow motion, reaching way up above their heads. For a split second, it remained transfixed in time, towering over them, its massive grey body glimmering in gold and red in the setting sun, majestically poised like a statue. Then it plummeted back, shattering the illusion.

Ben grabbed onto his paddleboard with all his might, bracing for impact.

Hao yelled in shock.

There was a colossal splash and the paddleboard somersaulted in the air before falling back into the water, ejecting Ben far below the surface, but closer to shore. For a moment he was lost in a silent, dark world of air bubbles and churning seawater before his life jacket pulled him upwards. He spluttered, gasping for breath.

There were cries for help as the motorboat groaned and tilted sideways dangerously. Already the whale breached for a second time, soaring above the ailing ship. A new shockwave sent them tumbling in all directions, submerging Ben again, while causing the motorboat to dangerously take in water.

Ben struggled to reach the surface. He had gulped in a good amount of water this time. His arms flailed desperately, while he tried to find his bearings. His hand fell on something soft. He blinked, trying to make out what it was.

It was Tike. The dog had come to his rescue.

Ben grabbed the dog's collar and let himself be pulled to the shore.

Laura and Mesmo ran up to him as the waves tossed him against the beach. "Ben!" his mother yelled, wading into the water to pull him out.

Susan joined them, then helped Laura drag Ben onto the shore. Laura sobbed and kissed his forehead as he hugged her back weakly. In the distance, the police motorboat lay on its side with half a dozen agents splashing in the water.

As Laura stroked her son's hair, Ben stared dazedly into the bay. He watched as the humpback whale slowly retreated into the distance, its tail sticking out of the water as if bidding him farewell.

Ben turned his attention to Mesmo, who stood nearby, gazing at him intently. Just before losing consciousness, he saw the alien break into a discreet smile.

He's proud of me!

CHAPTER 22 *The Shapeshifter*

After resting for two full days following Ben's escape at the lighthouse, both he and his mother made speedy recoveries in the cozy island cottage. Laura's appetite returned, while Ben was thrilled to find Tike again. He covered his dog in praise after hearing how his faithful companion had made it all the way back to Laura with the asthma inhaler clamped in his mouth.

That evening, Ben was heading out with a bucket and fishing rod when he caught sight of Mesmo's tall form on the pier. He had not seen the alien man since he had been pulled out of the water beneath the lighthouse. Ben ran over to him, Tike close at his heels.

"Mesmo!" Ben gasped, catching his breath.

"You're back!"

Mesmo smiled. "Yes," he said. "And I see you are feeling better."

Ben nodded. "If it hadn't been for that whale, I don't know what would have happened. Did you see that? How could it have known I needed help?" He spoke in wonder.

"Because you asked for help," Mesmo said matter-of-factly.

Ben frowned at his words. "Really?" he asked. "How? I don't remember doing that."

Mesmo smiled. "You don't realize your power yet. Your skill is barely beginning to take hold."

That smile again!

Mesmo's words made Ben feel uncomfortable. "You're proud of what happened, aren't you?" the boy quizzed.

"I am," Mesmo answered.

"Why?"

"Because I wasn't sure my daughter's skill would survive. But clearly, it has," he answered, still smiling.

He seems to think this is a good thing.

"What if..." Ben asked carefully, "...I don't want it?"

Mesmo's smile faded. "That question is

irrelevant," he replied. "It is part of you now. You should be happy."

Ben walked to the end of the pier to avoid Mesmo noticing that he did not share the alien's enthusiasm. He attached the hook to the end of the fishing line while he carefully thought about his next question. "What if the skill is making me sick?"

Mesmo went to stand beside him with a look of confusion on his face. "Sick?"

Ben shrugged, already regretting his question. He attached the bait to the hook, ignoring Mesmo's stare. Then the boy leaned back and threw the line far out into the dark water. "I didn't know you could fish for trout in the dark, did you?" Ben commented casually.

Mesmo wasn't letting him get away with a shrug as an answer. "Ben, what do you mean: the skill is making you sick?"

Ben sat down at the edge of the pier and sighed.

"It's nothing, really. I felt nauseous after encountering the whale. And there were seals, too." He wound up the spool and threw the line into the water again. "It was strange. In my mind, I was swimming with them under water. All I wanted to do was play with them. I forgot where I was and lost track of time. But when I came to, I felt so dizzy!"

Mesmo smiled again. His face relaxed. "Well, of course! You'd been floating on the ocean for hours! I'm not surprised you felt seasick!"

Ben didn't answer.

I knew you'd say that!

He anchored the fishing rod between two wooden planks so he wouldn't have to hold it and scratched Tike's head as the dog lay down on his lap contentedly.

What about the ants? I wasn't on the ocean then!

Ben didn't want to talk about this supposedly fabulous skill anymore. The alien obviously had no idea how uncomfortable the subject made him. While Mesmo was totally relaxed about it, Ben realized that the more he thought about this alien skill, the more afraid he became. It had been shoved on him without his consent, and he did not understand it.

They both gazed at the starry night until the fishing rod suddenly tensed. Ben grabbed at it and expertly caught a decent sized trout, which he placed in the bucket. He wasn't smiling when he saw his prize, though. "I used to go fishing with Grampa," he said softly, remembering.

Mesmo observed the trout, then said, "Ryan was a good man."

"How do you know? You barely even met him!" Ben quizzed. He sat down on the edge of the pier again and pulled up the side of his jacket collar so that Mesmo wouldn't notice he had closed his eyes tight. A part of him regretted having caught the fish.

"Actually, I did," Mesmo replied. "I went back to his house a couple of times between my travels. We spoke about many things, including how to best protect you."

Ben remained silent, concentrating on Mesmo's words to ignore a wave of nausea. Instead, he pictured his grandfather and Mesmo making plans about him. Thinking about his grandfather suddenly reminded him of something. "I meant to tell you," he said. "Bordock was at the hospital on the night Grampa died."

Mesmo's eyes widened. "Are you sure?"

"Yes. He was also at the Police Department. Did you know he works for the CSIS? How is that possible? How can the police not know he's an imposter?"

Mesmo remained thoughtful for a while, then said, "He has shifted. He has taken on the appearance of another human." He looked at Ben.

"I think this would be a good time to finish recovering your memories from the night of *The Cosmic Fall.*"

Ben frowned. "What do you mean? I thought we had done that already."

Mesmo bent over the side of the pier and placed his hand in the water. A soft, blue light emanated from the palm of his hand. The water responded by streaming upwards from the surface until a round, flat screen of transparent liquid took shape in front of the pier.

Mesmo sat beside Ben again, his hand outstretched as he maintained the liquid screen before them. His voice sounded bleak as he said, "You need to go back to the night I crashed. We need to find out what happened after my daughter passed away."

Ben stared hesitantly from Mesmo to the floating screen. He bit his lip, then reached out to touch the water with the tip of his fingers. He closed his eyes and was thrust back to the night of *The Cosmic Fall.*

* * *

"Mesmo," the girl murmured as she closed her eyes for the last time.

"No!" Ben shouted, reaching for her, but her body had slipped out of reach.

Ben stumbled away from the wreckage, sobbing. He held his right hand up before his face, slowly uncurling his fist, and in the fire-lit sky, saw that he was no longer bleeding. Instead, in the middle of his palm lay a glimmering gem. It reminded him of his mother's pretty diamond ring, the one she never wanted to wear and kept at the very back of a bathroom drawer.

"Benjamin!" he heard his grandfather gasp behind him. Grampa ran up to him, terrified. "Oh, my gosh, are you all right?" He pulled Ben to his feet. "What are you doing here, Potatohead?" He usually used that name when he was joking. Not this time. His brow tightened as he said angrily, "I told you to go to the house!"

"The house went dark," Ben argued. "There's a blackout."

Grampa muttered something under his breath, lifted a silent Tike up from the ground and pulled Ben away from the remains of the craft.

"Wait!" Ben objected. His Grampa paid no heed.

"This isn't right," Ben heard his Grampa mutter. "Something's not right." He froze in his tracks.

Ben bumped into him and glanced around his grandfather to find out why they had stopped. He gasped.

A tall man stood before them, surrounded by burning debris. He was shrouded in darkness, so they could not see his face. He did not move but kept his shining eyes on them. He had wavy, white hair. It was Mesmo.

Grampa held on tightly to Ben, ready to run, alert for any sign of danger.

Mesmo swayed. His legs gave way, and he crashed to the ground.

Grampa didn't wait to find out more. He was already running, pulling at Ben's wrist to keep going.

"Grampa!" Ben yelled. "Wait, Grampa! We've gotta help him!"

Grampa stared at him in surprise, hesitated, then looked back at the fallen man. Slowly, he approached the stranger. Grampa shoved at him gently with his foot, so they could see his face. It was streaked with dirt, while his hair was pure white.

Grampa lifted Mesmo over his shoulder until the man's head and arms were dangling over his back. He groaned with effort, teetering under the weight. He stabilized himself, got a better grasp around the man's waist, and lumbered away from the scene of the accident; Ben following his every footstep with Tike safely tucked into his jacket.

After a long and tedious time, they arrived at the house. Grampa pushed through the kitchen door and headed for the living room. There, he dumped Mesmo onto the couch like an old potato sack, then sagged to his knees, panting.

Ben put a hand on his shoulder worriedly. Grampa nodded to say he was fine. When he had caught his breath, he stood, and both stared at the mysterious man on the couch.

Ben took his grandfather's arm.

"Grampa," he said softly. "There are others."

Grampa stared at his grandson in amazement. He nodded slowly, answering in a distant voice, "I know. I saw them."

"We must help them!" Ben stated. The boy squeezed his grandfather's arm. "It's okay. I'll stay here." Ben nodded reassuringly, "I'll be okay."

Grampa nodded back. Without a word, he headed outside again. His shoulders slumped as though he were still carrying a heavy weight.

Ben tried the phone, though he knew the line would be dead. He headed to the kitchen window to watch his grandfather cross the field once more. He watched even after he had disappeared into the trees, following him in his mind's eye as he would reach the first crash site.

Maybe he'll find the girl.

Ben absentmindedly rubbed the palm of his hand, suddenly remembering the small diamond he was still clasping in his other hand. Tiny sparkles of light emanated from it. He stared at it in awe as it began to glow.

The window panes rattled alarmingly, making Ben jump and drop the jewel, which rolled under the kitchen sink. Tike bared his teeth as he crouched low.

Something was happening outside, in the field right before the house. A dark spacecraft descended slowly to the ground, about twenty meters away. It was black as the night and had a sleek form. It hovered a meter above the earth, humming softly, each hum sending an invisible wave that rattled the windows.

Then it went silent.

Ben froze to the spot, his throat dry and the hairs on the back of his neck prickled. The night was silent, expectant, and he hardly dared to breathe.

From some invisible opening in the craft, the form of a man appeared. He had spiky, white hair. Judging by his strong build, he could not have been very old. He was too far away for Ben to distinguish anything else, but for some reason, he broke into a cold sweat. No matter how much he longed to hide, he was rooted to the spot. He was afraid the slightest movement would alert the man to his presence.

Then an unexpected sound caught the attention of them both. The sirens from a police car swiftly approached on the road from town.

The alien from the spacecraft stood alert for an instant, listening, then after confirming the siren was approaching, the being ran straight for the house.

The spikey-haired man reached the bushes below Ben's window just as the headlights from the police car illuminated the house. The car came to a stop on the gravel before the front door, the whirling red and blue lights on its roof splashing across the lawn.

Agent Theodore Edmond Connelly stepped out. He spoke into the radio, listened as a woman's voice gave him instructions, then shut the car door and jogged towards the house.

Ben could hear the police officer's footsteps on the gravel as he approached before he banged on the front door. The noise shook Ben to the bone. "This is the police. Open the door! Mr. Archer, are you there?"

Ben's heart pounded. He sensed the presence of the man lurking below, like a spider in a web waiting to catch its prey.

After a moment, the sounds of footsteps on the gravel told Ben the police officer was moving away from the front door. He stopped for an instant before breaking into a run over the lawn. Ben peeked and could see the police officer freezing as he took in the dark spaceship. His hand was on the gun at his side, but he was too dumbfounded by what he was seeing to remember his own safety.

In the distance, more sirens wailed. The police officer turned to head for his car when he noticed something in the bushes behind him.

Ben opened his mouth in warning, but his voice was paralyzed in his throat. He heard the police officer yell, "Hold it!" as he reached for his gun—too late. He was struck by a sudden ray of intense blue light. Ben heard him groan as he tumbled to the ground.

The dark form materialized from the bushes under the window, running toward the dead man. Hastily, the murderer placed his hand an inch above Connelly's face until a blue light emanated from it, enveloping them both. Before his very eyes, Ben saw the white-haired being's face transform and take on the bald police officer's traits. Ben could tell that the alien was in great pain as this was happening. His mouth twisted and the muscles of his body bulged abnormally beneath the clothes. As the transformation completed, the eerie blue light faded away. In a swift movement, the murderer heaved the dead man's body on his shoulder and carried him to the spaceship, where both disappeared. Shortly after, the fake Theodore Connelly reappeared in full police garments, his victim still inside the spacecraft. He ran to the middle of the field when a helicopter flew overhead, its powerful searchlight illuminating the ground. Ben saw the murderer with Connelly's face gaze up to the house with its eyes that were two pools of darkness that carved themselves into Ben's mind.

Twisted eyes!

Then several things happened at once. Mesmo, who, a moment ago, had been lying unconscious on Grampa's couch, placed a firm hand on Ben's mouth, pulling him down. The lights of the house sprang back to life. The helicopter hovered over the police officer who was shielding his eyes with his arm. Several police cars, ambulances and firefighters made a dramatic entrance onto the road next to the field, as the night came ablaze with noise and flashing lights.

* * *

The liquid screen lost its consistency and returned from where it had come with a splash.

Ben backed away, breathing heavily. He stared at Mesmo with wide eyes.

"You passed out," Mesmo explained. "I carried you out of the house and ran all night until we reached the town. I left you under a tree, close to some houses, and sent Tike to look for help. Then I left."

Alien and boy stared silently at the dark inlet, lost in thought.

Tike pricked his ears. They followed the dog's gaze and found Laura walking towards them, her hands stuffed deep into her jacket pockets to fend off the cold.

"Any luck?" she asked cheerfully.

Ben stood hastily and handed her the bucket with the trout's head sticking out of it. "I'm turning vegetarian," he said gloomily.

Laura laughed, then noticed her son's sunken eyes. "What's the matter?" she asked worriedly.

"Tired," he muttered. "Going to bed." He trudged off toward the cabin with the fishing rod.

Laura followed him with her eyes, then turned to Mesmo. "What happened?" She asked, holding the bucket tightly in her arms.

"He'll be fine," the alien replied grimly.

She studied the alien as they headed back to the cabin. She noticed the grayish tint on his skin. She stopped and said softly, "What about you? We haven't had a chance to talk. Are you all right?"

He turned his head towards her. "I am better, yes."

She pulled out a hand from her pocket and gently weaved it through his own. There was only empty air where her eyes saw a firm hand. She held her breath, then said, "Ben told me about your troubles. He said you are being held against your will." She looked up at him again. "What happened to you?"

He stared at her grimly as they began walking again. His voice sounded pained. "I was kidnapped at the Toronto Airport. The man who is responsible for holding me knows that I am not from this planet. He is the head of a powerful organization, I can tell."

"A government agency?" Laura ventured.

Mesmo shook his head. "No. I don't think so. This is something else. I have not been able to figure it out yet."

Laura said, "We will help you in any way we can."

Mesmo shook his head again. "That would not be a good idea. You are safe here. Leaving this island would be too risky."

She noticed the dark rings under his eyes. "You don't look well, Mesmo..." she said softly.

He grimaced. "They placed me in a confined space. It is the one thing my species dreads." He glanced at Laura. "I couldn't take it. My heart stopped. They were able to revive me, but I barely made it..."

Laura gaped at his words. "Mesmo!" she breathed, her eyes wide. She stood before him to get his full attention. "Don't give up!" she said determinedly. "We'll find you and get you out, I promise."

Mesmo smiled sadly. "What Ben is doing for me is enough already. His spirit portal allows me to escape my jail briefly, even if it is only part of me. The man who is holding me has gone away for several months. That will give me some time to recover and find a way to escape." He trailed off and looked up at the night sky.

Laura gazed up as well, then said, "I meant to thank you, for taking care of Ben. Ever since the events in Chilliwack, he's been so afraid, so fragile. But he's changing. I can see it. He's becoming more confident by the day. You do that to him. He trusts you." She smiled. "So for that, thank you."

The door to the cabin opened, and light splashed onto the lawn. Susan let them in and took the bucket from Laura. "Here, let me get that," she said. "You go on up and get some rest."

Laura nodded and smiled shyly at Mesmo. "Well, goodnight then," she said, her eyes on him, before turning away.

Susan dumped the fish into the kitchen sink. She washed it energetically before cutting it open, then removed its entrails, while Mesmo watched curiously. After a long silence, she said coolly, "Still playing with their hearts, are we?"

Mesmo straightened. "I need them, just as much as they need me."

Susan eyed him with displeasure. "Yes, but who's going to get their feelings trampled on in the end?" She shoved the fish into the freezer, then peeled off her latex gloves. "You?" she asked accusingly.

CHAPTER 23 *Flight*

Two weeks later Ben woke up to a misty morning. He found Susan bustling about in the kitchen, making breakfast. She had spent almost an entire day on the mainland the day before, returning with loads of fresh food. The whole house smelled of eggs and bacon. Ben checked in with his mother to see if she was ready to come and eat.

Laura awoke, stretching lazily. Ben grinned, noticing how much better she looked: her cheeks were rosy, she had put on some much-needed weight, and she looked rested.

She smiled at him. "'Morning, honey," she said as she patted the bed to invite him to sit beside her, noticing that his mood had significantly improved over the past weeks.

He did so reluctantly, his stomach grumbling. He leaned back and stared at the ceiling. "It's as if we were on vacation or something," Ben commented.

Laura turned to face him, saying cheekily, "Well, technically, it's the middle of the term. We need to find a way to get you back to school."

Ben stared at her in horror. "Are you serious?"

Laura poked him in the side. "Dead serious."

"Ouch! No way!" Ben objected, half giggling. In defense, he grabbed a pillow and hit her gently on the head as she poked him playfully in the side again. That only triggered more pillow fighting. They both giggled until Mesmo appeared in the doorway. They stopped midway in their fight, their hair in a mess, grinning sheepishly as the alien man stared at them with utter bewilderment.

"Well, don't just stand there!" Laura said as she threw a pillow at him, forgetting that he wasn't really there. The pillow went right through him, landing on the other side of the doorway. Ben fell backwards on the bed, laughing uncontrollably.

"Oops!" Laura said, putting a hand to her mouth.

Mesmo frowned. "What are you doing?"

Laura wiped away the tears at the corner of her eyes as she tried to control her laughter. "We're being foolish, is all. Don't you ever have laughing fits where you come from?"

"No, of course not," he said. "Why would you want to do something that makes you cry?"

Ben guffawed, placing a pillow over his face.

"That's enough, Ben," Laura warned, putting a hand on his shoulder with a smile still on her face. Addressing Mesmo, she said, "Sometimes people cry from happiness. It's very liberating. You should try it sometime."

Mesmo shook his head in disagreement. "We learned, long ago, that excessive emotions were the root of many wars. Strong displays of emotion are considered barbaric."

Laura's smile wavered. She gazed at Mesmo with renewed interest, then asked carefully, "Is there... family... waiting for you back home?"

Mesmo shook his head.

Ben, who recovered from his laughing fit, stared at him quizzically, blurting, "What? Don't you have a wife or something?"

"Ben!" Laura growled from the corner of her mouth, her face flushed.

Ben blushed immediately. "Sorry!" he mumbled, realizing that this conversation had taken an awkward turn.

The alien man answered, "If by 'wife,' you mean a life companion, then, yes, I had a 'wife.' She died not long ago."

Laura and Ben stared at him, suddenly silenced. "I'm sorry," Laura said earnestly, before adding slowly, "Perhaps one day you will remarry."

Mesmo frowned. "What is 'remarry'?"

"Er..." Laura struggled. "It means to take another wife. Find another... 'life companion.'"

Mesmo shook his head. "That is not possible! We are matched once in our life. There can be no other."

"Ugh!" Ben said, suddenly losing interest. "I smell waffles."

He leapt off the bed, then said, "Excuse me!" as he waited for Mesmo to move aside and let him through. Technically, Ben could have walked right through the alien, but for some reason, that seemed inappropriate.

"Are you coming?" the white-haired man asked Laura, who had fallen silent.

"Yes, yes," she said, waving him on. "I'll be right there."

He nodded, looking at her curiously, then followed Ben to the kitchen.

Laura stared at the floor, lost in thought. She was no longer smiling.

* * *

Breakfast lifted their spirits. Laura feasted her eyes on the well laid-out table full of fresh bread, eggs, bacon, waffles, jam and fruit.

"Thank you, Susan!" she exclaimed. "I don't know how we can ever repay you!"

"Sit down and eat a hearty breakfast. You'll be needing it." Susan ordered sternly.

Laura obeyed. "I'm going to have to find work. We can't go on like this. We've run out of money."

"Oh!" Ben exclaimed through a mouthful of waffle. "We still have some money. Well, sort of." He plunged his hand into his jeans pocket, fishing out something small and holding it up in the palm of his hand. Swallowing, he said, "Dad's ring."

Laura started, turning red. "What? How...?"

"I found it back home, in the bathroom drawer. I figured if you never wore it, maybe we could sell it."

Laura hastily took the engagement ring from him, throwing an embarrassed look at Susan and Mesmo.

Mesmo pointed at the ring in her hand. "Your… life companion?"

"I…" she began.

"Dad gave it to her so they could get married," Ben interrupted, munching on some grapes. "He died in a car crash when I was a baby." An awkward silence fell on the table, though Ben was in too good a mood to notice. "Show me the flower trick again, Mesmo! Please?" he begged as he helped himself to some more bacon.

Laura slipped the ring into her own pocket, relieved to change the subject, then filled her plate as she watched Mesmo touch the surface of a jug of water. The liquid obeyed his command, flowing into a complex bouquet of delicate, transparent flowers, the stems gently swaying to an invisible breeze, the thin petals turning a glistening silver as they froze.

Ben gasped in wonder, his eyes twinkling. Laura smiled gratefully at Mesmo, then glanced at Susan to see if she approved. The older woman was staring at her untouched plate with a sullen face.

"Susan?" Laura said, concerned. "What's the matter?"

The unsmiling woman lifted her eyes, then said darkly, "You are going to have to leave." She had spoken in a low voice, yet they all heard her loud and clear.

Laura coughed up the grape she was trying to swallow. Mesmo lost his concentration, and the watery flowers splashed onto the table. Ben stopped chatting, turning his attention to his mother questioningly. They stared at their host, wondering if they had heard her correctly. They waited for Susan to admit she was making a distasteful joke. Instead, she glanced at them and insisted, "You heard me. You're going to have to leave. Today!"

There was a long, uncomfortable silence. Laura cleared her throat. "Hum. Yes. Of course! We have long outstayed our visit. You have treated us so well, Susan, that we sort of lost track of the fact that we were invading your home and your privacy."

Susan rested her forehead in her hand, her elbow on the table. "That's not it," she began. She stared at them guiltily, before continuing, "I called both my sons yesterday afternoon, while I was in Deep Cove. I'd been resisting the urge to do so for quite some time. I think of my sons every single day, but having you around somehow reminded me how much I missed being able to touch them, to hear their voices, to hug them… They are both married. My youngest had his second baby last month." She broke down into tears. "I can't live like this anymore. I need to see them. I need to see them so bad it hurts," she sobbed.

Laura hurried to her side to hug her. Susan sniffled before adding, "I'm meeting them in Deep Cove this afternoon."

Mesmo cautioned, "They won't be the only ones meeting you there, Susan."

"Don't you think I know that?" she retorted. "Don't you think I know my son's phones are bugged? That a hundred prying ears overheard every word we said?" She shook her head as she blew her nose on a napkin. "I don't care. I don't care anymore. They can arrest me, jail me, accuse me of god-knows-what. But I want to see my sons."

A new silence settled heavily among them, as each realized the consequences of Susan's action. Their hiding place was compromised. Danger loomed closer to their doorstep with every passing minute.

"You saved our lives, Susan. We will be forever grateful for that. But you must go and see your sons, no matter what," Laura said. For the first time, she dared look into Ben's wide eyes, then said determinedly, "We will pack our bags and leave. If you could drop us somewhere on the mainland, we'll disappear from your life."

Somewhere above the cabin, they heard the roaring of an airplane.

Susan sniffled again. "That won't be necessary."

* * *

Tike scampered outside, followed closely by Ben. They rushed out onto the grass to watch the small hydroplane as it descended onto the inlet. It broke through the last clinging mist as it landed, then headed straight for the island.

Laura and Mesmo caught up with them, anxiously trying to make out who was inside the plane. The motor spluttered as the pilot slowly maneuvered the craft next to the pier before coming to a final stop. The plane bobbed up and down. They could see the pilot moving about inside as he prepared to exit.

Susan stepped out of her wooden cabin. Smiling, she said, "Don't worry, he's a friend."

Laura relaxed while Ben ran after his dog, excited to study a hydroplane up close. Susan followed the boy towards the pier where a dark-skinned man with a very thick, knee-length, winter jacket, stepped out of the plane. Immediately, he proceeded to remove the cumbersome piece of clothing.

Laura and Mesmo watched from afar as their host greeted the middle-aged man who was wearing jeans and a black sweater. He hugged Susan. Then they talked for a moment before the man turned his attention to Ben and Tike. He shook the boy's hand, then patted the small terrier, whose tongue lolled in a canine laugh.

Ben sprinted back to his mother. Grinning, he said, "I know who he is!" Instead of explaining further, he ran into the house, leaving Laura and Mesmo clueless.

Susan and the newcomer walked slowly over to them, still chatting somberly until they came face to face. Susan introduced them. "This is Thomas Nombeko, originally from Chilliwack. Thomas, this is Laura Archer—Ryan Archer's daughter. And this is... er... Jack Anderson."

Thomas Nombeko shook Laura's hand while he eyed Mesmo with a touch of fear in his eyes. Nervously, he held out his hand to greet Mesmo the same way. Susan pulled it down, indicating he shouldn't insist.

Ben came rushing out again. Breathless, he said, "He's on Grampa's list!"

He proudly held out the small, brown envelope which he handed to his mother, who frowned as she peered inside, then took out the crumpled notebook page containing the list of five people in Grampa's handwriting.

"See?" Ben said, pointing to Susan's name. "This is how I contacted Susan. And here's Thomas Nombeko. They were all Grampa's contacts."

Laura recognized the names on the list: Ben Archer was her father, Susan Pickering was their host, Wayne McGuillen was the homeless man from Chilliwack, and Thomas Nombeko was standing before them. "You are all witnesses!" she exclaimed, suddenly connecting the dots.

Thomas Nombeko nodded. "Yes. I used to be a mailman in Chilliwack. I lived not too far from your father's house. I even saw your father and Ben on the night of *The Cosmic Fall*. I was cycling home that night and spotted them out on the field," he said. Then addressing Ben, he added, "You probably don't remember that."

Ben looked down at his feet.

I remember.

Not wanting to linger on the memory, he pointed to the last name on the list. "This Bob M. must be another witness."

Susan and Thomas both stared at the last name on the list, then shook their heads, confused.

"I've never heard of him," Susan pondered. "Come, let's go inside. There isn't much time. You must get packing. Thomas here has offered to take you to a safe place."

"Really?" Ben said excitedly. "Where are we going? Are we flying?" Ben had already taken a liking to the fourty-something-year-old man, who had a soft demeanour and a contagious laugh.

"We are flying, yes."

"Whoa!" Susan interrupted. "You promised, Thomas, not a word about where you're going. I don't want to know."

They stepped into the house, chatting happily.

* * *

Laura stayed behind. Her face had become drawn as she stared blankly at the names on the notebook page. She jumped when she realized Mesmo stood silently behind her. Guiltily, she folded the sheet three times so it would fit in her back pocket. "I'd better hang on to this," she said in a shaky voice. "Might come in handy." She smiled without meeting his eyes, then headed inside.

Soon they were packed and ready to go. Ben, Mesmo and Tike were already headed to the hydroplane with Thomas, who was diligently explaining how the craft functioned.

Laura checked the log cabin one last time to make sure they hadn't forgotten anything, though they were travelling light as they had become stranded without any belongings. Susan had managed to buy them some emergency clothing and toiletries, but that was about all they had.

Laura approached Susan, who waited by the doorway. "Will you be all right?" she asked.

The woman had become somber, yet she gazed at Laura with determined eyes. "You don't have to worry about me. I'm a survivor. Nothing could be worse than what I've already been through. Though this time I'll have my sons near me. I know they will defend me in any way they can." She paused before adding, "And anyway, it's not me they want..."

Laura said carefully, "Susan, if they catch you, I want you to tell them everything you know."

Susan stared at her in surprise.

"Listen to me," Laura urged, taking her

hand. "Mesmo has many enemies. One, in particular, is extremely dangerous. He will do anything to get to Mesmo. He will know if you are lying or holding back information. So don't hold anything back. The main thing is that you don't know where Thomas Nombeko is taking us, so we will be safe."

Susan nodded. She checked to make sure the others were out of earshot, before saying, "I have something to tell you as well." She led Laura to the fireplace, where she picked up an envelope off its shelf. She handed it to Laura. "When the government agents released us, your father gave me this letter and asked me to give it to you, were we ever to meet."

It was Laura's turn to stare at Susan as she accepted the envelope.

Susan held onto Laura's hands. "Be careful, Laura. We don't know who this Mesmo is. Not really." She hesitated before adding, "Don't let him break your heart." She let go of Laura, then headed out before the other could object.

Once Susan was gone, Laura tore open the envelope. She carefully read the letter inside. For a long time, she stood in the middle of the living room, holding her father's letter close to her chest, her cheeks wet with tears. Finally, she dried her eyes, breathed deeply, threw the letter in the dying embers of the fireplace, and waited for it to catch fire. She stepped out of the cabin, closed the door for the last time, and went to join her son who had boarded the hydroplane with Mesmo, Thomas and Tike.

Before long they had taken flight, swooping over the tiny island, the shimmering inlet, and Susan Pickering who was waving goodbye from the pier. They soared up over the majestic, snow-capped mountain ranges that went on and on for as far as the eye could see, heading towards an unknown destination.

EPILOGUE

"My Dearest Honeybee,

(You are to destroy this letter as soon as you have read it.)

If you are reading these words, then it means I have failed you.

I have tried, by all means possible, to protect you and Ben from falling under the radar of some treacherous people so that you could lead a normal life. But if you have met Susan Pickering and she has given you this letter, then it means all my efforts were in vain. It means you and Ben are in grave danger and that, for whatever reason, I can be with you no longer.

Please understand, my Honeybee, that meeting with you would have meant drawing all kinds of prying eyes your way. I had to avoid that at all costs. No matter what, you must not let anyone lay their hands on Ben. I swear, Laura, if secret agents catch him they will never let him go. They all want the same thing: they want to know about the aliens that crashed in Chilliwack on the night of The Cosmic Fall. They want to know about their technology, their planet, their intentions, their WEAPONS...

You'd think it would be for scientific reasons and for the advancement of the human race. But no, they are power-hungry egoists intent on dominating their fellow human beings.

If you found Susan, then you will have gotten my list. You can trust all the names on that list. I insist: ALL of them. Even the last one. You know who I mean...

There is also another who you can trust. His name is Mesmo. He crashed in my backyard on the night of The Cosmic Fall and survived. I have spoken to him many times during his short visits. I know he will protect you because I saved his life. I pray he will have found his way to you. Beware, Laura, Mesmo's mission on Earth is greater than our understanding, and he will crush you if he feels you are standing in his way.

Yet, I know you, my angel, and even an otherworldly creature could not resist your kindness. You may be our only hope!

You have already met Mesmo. You met him on that fateful day when you came looking for me in Chilliwack. I was there, Laura. I was hiding from you. I could not let you in, no matter how much I ached to. But I swear, I was holding you in my arms the whole time you were talking to Mesmo on the doorstep, and I never wanted to let you go.

I hope you will find it in your heart to forgive me because I cannot forgive myself.

I love you, always,

Dad

THE ADVENTURE CONTINUES:

Ben Archer and the Alien Skill
(The Alien Skill Series, Book 2)
https://www.amazon.com/dp/1989605095

LEAVE A REVIEW:

If you enjoyed this book, please leave a review in the 'Write a customer review' section:

https://www.amazon.com/dp/1989605192

PREQUEL:

Read the prequel to The Alien Skill Series,
The Great War of the Kins:

www.raeknightly.com

The Alien Skill Series continues!

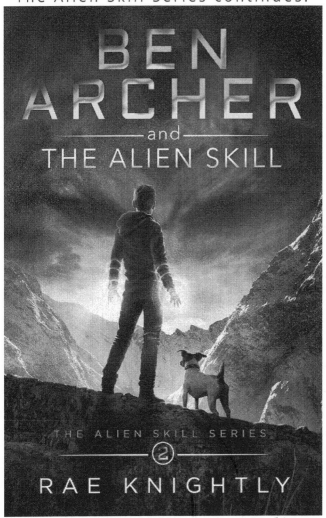

BEN ARCHER
and
THE ALIEN SKILL

THE ALIEN SKILL SERIES

2

RAE KNIGHTLY

Turn the page and start reading…

CHAPTER 1 *The Spacecraft*

Once more, Inspector James Hao found himself staring at the final report containing the results of the blood sample. No matter how hard he tried to make sense of it, the evidence remained undeniable: the individual the sample had been extracted from was not a human being.

Hao couldn't believe that, a little over a month ago, he had been sitting opposite the subject in the interrogation room of the Vancouver Police Department. Never would the Inspector have suspected that, behind the innocent features of a twelve-year-old boy, lay a creature from another planet. Hao's stomach twisted at the thought.

A week ago, High Inspector George Tremblay, Head of the National Aerial Division of the CSIS, had tapped the file with the tips of his fingers. "This file remains between us," he had said, eyeing Hao and his colleague, Connelly. The three men had stood in the High Inspector's office, facing each other.

Tremblay had lifted an eyebrow at Connelly. "You took the sample without my prior authorization. I should fire you for acting in such an unprofessional manner. You can consider yourself lucky that your hunch about the subject was correct. Nevertheless, this information will not enter the official investigation and is not to be mentioned beyond this office. The fact that this child, this Benjamin Archer, is an extraterrestrial must remain between us. Is that clear?"

Hao had observed Connelly out of the corner of his eye, secretly satisfied to watch his colleague being reprimanded by their chief. Even though he had taken a dislike to his colleague and had personnally disapproved of the blood extraction, he had to hand it to Connelly for getting results. All in all, he had to admit that Connelly's methods of investigation were particularly efficient if not particularly legal.

The cell phone on Hao's desk buzzed,

pulling him out of his thoughts. A message arrived, accompanied by a tiny image. Hao's forehead—creased in concentration a second ago—softened, and a chuckle escaped his lips. He pressed the image to enlarge it, and the huge, black nuzzle of an English Shephard appeared. The black dog was checking out the camera of whoever was taking the picture.

The message read: DID YOU FORGET ME?

Hao smiled and checked his watch. It was close to midnight at the Dugout, located in Eastern Canada, which meant it was nine pm where the message had originated.

What am I doing, still stuck at my desk at this hour? Hao brooded.

He hesitated for an instant, then pressed on the message to dial the number. The phone rang once before someone picked up, and a woman's voice answered in surprise, "Hello?"

"Hi, Lizzie," Hao said.

"Jimmy?" the woman said. There was shuffling in the background and Hao heard Lizzie's muffled voice, "Still! Sit still, Buddy!" Then her voice sounded clearer. "Oh my gosh! You should see that! He knows it's you! Yes, Buddy! It's your daddy! Your long-lost daddy..."

Hao heard the English Shephard bark

happily, and he was reminded people lived normal, tranquil lives out in the real world.

"Jimmy?" Lizzie began. "I can't believe it's you. I sent that picture of Buddy, but never thought you'd actually have time to call back. Must be my lucky day!"

Hao grinned. "How are you, Sis?"

Lizzie sighed in an exaggerated manner. "Do I really need to tell you? Buddy uprooted my rosebushes this afternoon. You know how we love him around here, but, honestly, I love my flowers more."

Hao could hear Buddy panting in the background.

Lizzie continued, "I haven't heard from you in ages! When are you coming home?"

Hao's mood darkened as his eyes slid back to the blood file on his desk. "Not anytime soon. I've got a big case on my hands. Probably the biggest I'll ever work on." He sighed. "I realize Buddy's a burden for you. Do you want me to contact the dog kennel we talked about?"

Lizzie remained silent for a moment, before answering earnestly, "Of course not. I love my roses, but if it helps you, then I'm happy to keep Buddy for a bit longer. You know Geoffrey and I wouldn't want to see him cooped up and miserable."

Hao let out a silent breath of relief. "Thanks. I owe you one. When this is over, we'll go pick out some rose-bushes together."

"You?" Lizzie scoffed. "In a plant nursery? Never gonna happen!"

They both laughed.

"Seriously, Jimmy," Lizzie said with a concerned voice. "There's always a new case popping up. You make it sound as if you were the only one catching the bad guys. I know I'm repeating myself, but bad guys will be around with or without you. And, trust me, there's a dozen younger James Bonds out there longing to take your place."

Hao scoffed, "Take it easy, Sis, I'm not that old!"

Lizzie clicked her tongue which meant to him that she wasn't ready to crack jokes. She pushed on. "If you were still married, your wife would be the one scolding you instead of me. So brace yourself while I nag you for a bit!"

Hao stood with a knowing smile. He paced along the office window overlooking a cavernous hangar and let her have her moment.

"I know how important it is to you to put the criminals behind bars and I, more than anyone, appreciate how hard you work to keep we little citizens safe," Lizzie spoke. "But, you have to stop acting like you're the only one carrying the burden." Her voice sounded thick with worry as she added, "I just want to make sure you stop in time."

While he listened, Hao gazed at the impressive, alien spacecraft that hovered a few feet from the concrete floor at the center of the dim hangar. Everyone, except for security, had left for the night. Only a couple of emergency and forgotten office lights illuminated the area. He thought he saw a movement blend into the shadow cast by the spacecraft and leaned forward, forgetting the phone stuck to his ear.

Lizzie's concerned voice came through to him again. "I know you. You wouldn't call unless something was wrong. Is something the matter?"

Since nothing moved in the grey hangar, except for his own reflection in his office window, Hao's well-built frame relaxed, and he turned to head back to his desk.

"Jimmy? Are you listening?" she asked.

"Hm, yeah, I'm listening," he replied with a tired voice. He sat back in his office chair and rubbed his left temple as he shut his eyes. He needed to rest, but the case wouldn't let him go.

And suddenly he realized why.

"It's weird," he said thoughtfully, speaking more to himself than his sister. "You know me: you know I'm an expert at telling good from bad, right? I mean, I understand the mind of a murderer; I know how to pick out a crook; I'm always a step ahead of elaborate thieves. I catch them and put them behind bars, where they belong." He broke off, picking up the file in front of him. "But these ones, Lizzie? Jeez, for all I know, they could start World War Three tomorrow, and I wouldn't even suspect." He shook his head, surprised at his own confession. "The thing is, for the first time in my career, I've been asked to chase down criminals I don't understand." He paused. "And that frightens me."

Continue reading
Ben Archer and the Alien Skill
(The Alien Skill Series, Book 2)
https://www.amazon.com/dp/1989605095

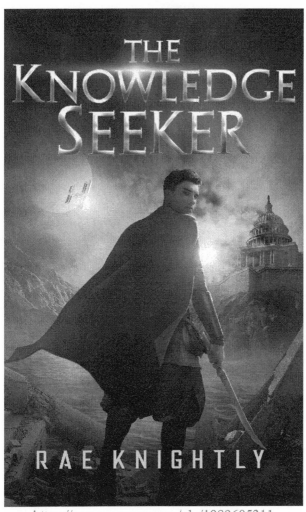

https://www.amazon.com/ dp/1989605311

About the Author

Rae Knightly invites the young reader on a journey into the imagination, where science fiction and fantasy blend into the real world. Young heroes are taken on gripping adventures full of discovery and story twists.

Rae Knightly lives in Vancouver with her husband and two children. The breathtaking landscapes of British Columbia have inspired her to write The Alien Skill Series.

Follow Rae Knightly on social media:
Facebook/Instagram/Twitter/Pinterest
E-mail: raeknightly@gmail.com

Acknowledgments

To my husband, for believing in me.
To my parents, for opening my eyes to the world.
To my children, for the stars in their eyes.
To Cristy, for her positive mentorship.

To you, reader, for taking the time to read
Ben Archer and the Cosmic Fall.

Thank you!
Rae Knightly

Made in the USA
Las Vegas, NV
10 November 2022

59170196R00199